Unlucky in Love

Unlucky in Love

JILL SANDERS

Montlake
Romance

Published by Montlake Romance, Seattle

www.apub.com

Amazon, the Amazon logo, and Montlake Romance are trademarks of Amazon.com, Inc., or its affiliates.

ISBN-13: 9781503933293
ISBN-10: 1503933296

Cover design by Shasti O'Leari Soudant

Printed in the United States of America

To my wonderful man,
who's made me a very lucky woman . . .

PROLOGUE

Kristen Collins was in love. Not just love, but LOVE. Sure, she was only eight years old and her best friend, Amelia, kept trying to tell her that Bobby Hurst was a no-good, booger-picking boy. She didn't care. She was in love.

Maybe it was the way Bobby walked or the fact that he always smiled at her, even though he was still missing his right front tooth. It could have had to do with his deep blue eyes; Kristen was a sucker for blue eyes. Anyway, Bobby was cute enough to win her third-grade heart for an entire week until Kristen saw him holding Jennifer Taylor's hand in the halls.

Amelia was there to help her through the rough spot and mend her broken heart, and Kristen learned a valuable lesson that day. Not only did boys lie, but they would come and go. The only thing that she could count on was Amelia's friendship, which was going to last forever.

CHAPTER ONE

Fifteen years later . . .

There weren't enough four-leaf clovers in the world to save her now, Kristen thought as the police photographer took what seemed like a hundred pictures of her new apartment. She leaned against the empty wall and felt like crying.

"Miss Collins?" A rather large female officer approached her from outside. "There is someone here to see you."

"Yes?" She turned and almost squealed when she saw Amy standing behind the woman.

Amelia Walker, Amy for short, had and always would be Kristen's best friend.

The two women looked like they would have nothing in common.

Amy was put together. Everything she did was perfect, down to her shiny toenails. She never had a hair out of place. It was how Amy had always been.

Kristen, for her part, looked more like a gypsy. Her clothes were bright and colorful, and usually turned a few heads in her direction. Amy always said it was Kristen's artistic side showing through.

For the last year and a half, Kristen had been fulfilling her lifelong dream of working as an interior designer for Row and Stein Architecture Firm in downtown Denver. With her imagination and her eye for color, the job was perfect for her. Plus, the firm was full of like-minded people with whom she got along great.

"I warned you about Rod." Amy pulled her into a quick hug, then handed Kristen a tissue.

"I know." She groaned and walked Amy into her empty apartment.

"Oh, Kristen!" Amy shook her head, sending her perfect hair swaying with the movement. She turned and hugged Kristen again. "I'm so sorry," she whispered into her ear. This time, Kristen did need the tissue.

"I suppose I should have seen this coming. You know, after the incident," she mumbled.

Amy rolled her eyes and crossed her arms over her chest. "There's no such thing as bad juju."

Kristen laughed sarcastically and motioned around the room.

Amy patted her on the arm. "This is not just bad luck in love. You picked a loser. You have a knack for picking losers."

"That's not true," she said as one of the police officers glanced her way. "Well," she whispered, "I guess this time you were right."

Amy started ticking off her fingers. "First it was Bobby what's-his-name."

"Hurst." Kristen supplied the last name.

"Right." Amy nodded. "Then Tom . . ." She glanced Kristen's way and waited.

"Swanson."

"Next it was Brian . . ."

"Barber."

Amy shook her head. "He was a real winner. Didn't he leave you in the mall parking lot at eleven at night when you wouldn't—" She broke off and made a vulgar motion with her fist.

Kristen almost laughed, but it had been truly scary standing in the Aurora Mall parking lot in the middle of the night until Amy had come and picked her up.

"Yeah." She frowned and looked down at her hands.

"You were sixteen. You could have been—" She took a deep breath. "Then it was Tyler." She threw up her hands. "Then . . . more guys than I can remember. And now, Rod." She sighed and looked around.

"I'm not one hundred percent sure that this was him." She motioned around her nearly empty apartment.

Amy continued to look at her in silence. Her eyes told Kristen exactly what she was thinking. Then she stopped a police officer who was walking past them out of the room.

"Was this a break-in?"

"No, ma'am. There isn't any forced entry. Besides, the lady next door gave us a description of Miss Collins's boyfriend as the one who was driving the U-Haul truck. He and two other men told her that Miss Collins was moving out."

She closed her eyes, wishing cops would keep their mouths shut. She'd heard the news forty minutes ago when her neighbor had told them the story in the first place.

Amy handed her another tissue from her purse.

"Well, don't worry. I've got plenty of room in my spare—"

Kristen shook her head. "I'm not staying at your place."

Amy frowned. "You're not staying here." She looked around.

"Why not? It's not like he's going to come back for the carpet," she said.

Amy chuckled, then looked Kristen in the eyes. They'd known each other long enough for Amy to know that she wasn't backing down. Finally, Amy conceded. "Fine, but you're having the locks changed, and we're going to go buy you some basics."

She quickly hugged her friend again.

After waiting an hour for the locksmith to install new locks on Kristen's apartment door, they headed out to the mall to get toiletries and some new clothes.

Three hours later, just as snow was starting to fall, they walked back up the stairs toward her apartment. It was an old building in an older part of downtown, and Kristen loved every inch of the place. Sure, the carpet was a little worn and it took five minutes for the water to heat up, but she wouldn't have traded it for the world. Especially when she looked out her living room windows and saw the panoramic view of Denver.

The Rockies spread from one side of the large windows to the next. Well, at least on days when it wasn't snowing or cloudy.

The apartment was minutes to her office and she loved riding the light rail every day, even when it was cold and snowy.

On their first stop, they had gone to a giant outdoor sporting goods store, and she was now the proud owner of an air mattress, a small digital alarm clock, and an extra-fluffy sleeping bag. Then they had gone to the mall downtown where they had started to make a dent in replacing her lost items. The jerk had even stolen most of her clothes. Amy had different taste in clothing than she did, which made clothes shopping with her interesting. Somehow, her friend always talked her into buying stuff that Kristen wouldn't have picked out for herself. Things that looked more professional. Tailored skirts, silk blouses—she'd even convinced her to buy a blazer. What was she going to do with a blazer?

"What do you think he wants with my shoes?" she asked as Amy helped her unload her items.

"Maybe he's really a cross-dresser and wanted a new wardrobe." Amy tried to hide a smile.

Kristen shrugged. "It would never work. I wear a size eight shoe, he's a size ten in men's."

They both laughed.

"It's going to take some time to replace everything." Kristen put her hands on her hips as she looked around her empty place. They had ~~bought two big beanbags for her living room.~~ The older television, which they had picked up from her mother's place, sat on a small table across the room. At least now she could sit back and relax comfortably until the insurance check arrived and she could afford a new sofa and more furniture.

"Don't worry; insurance will pay for most of it. We can make a run to the furniture store this weekend, if you want."

She thought about how much time she'd spent picking out her last furniture. Then she remembered she already had plans and stifled a groan. "I've got that thing with my folks."

"Oh right." Amy's parents had divorced when she was twelve, so she didn't have to attend monthly dinners with the two of them. But Kristen's folks, despite some drama recently, were still happily together. It made Kristen want to run in the opposite direction every time she had to sit through a hand-holding, kissy-face, monthly dinner. Even though her parents were legally separated, they had started dating each other again and acted like lovestruck teenagers around her.

She loved her parents, really. She just wished they would act their ages instead of like hormonal teenagers who needed to get a room.

"I'll go through my closet and drop off some clothes for you later this week."

"Don't you dare." She glared at her friend. "I know what that means."

"What?" Amy turned toward her and tried to look innocent.

"When you say, 'I'll go through my closet,' what you really mean is, 'I'll go clothes shopping for you and buy you what I think will look good on you.'"

"Oh, come on. It gives me a great excuse to go shopping. Besides, you look smoking in the blazer." Amy winked at her. "You're going to need so much. We only bought you three pairs of shoes." Amy held her hand over her forehead and faked a faint by rolling her eyes back.

She giggled. "*You* may need six dozen pairs of shoes, but *I* was happily content—" She stopped and gasped. "He took my UGGs!" She felt like crying all over again.

"Good riddance," Amy said under her breath, causing Kristen to narrow her eyes at her.

"I've had those since high school. They were my most comfortable—"

"Shabby, nasty looking things," Amy supplied. "Besides, you were due for a new pair. I can . . ."

"No." She turned and held up her hand to her friend. "I will buy my own wardrobe." Amy nodded, but Kristen knew there was no stopping the flow of clothing that would be coming her way.

"What about groceries?" Amy asked, walking into her kitchen. "Dishes?" She groaned as she opened the empty cabinets. "Man, he cleaned you out completely. Not that you had a lot of stuff." She glanced at Kristen over her shoulder.

"I was working on it. Besides, I enjoyed finding everything I had."

It was true; Kristen loved finding unique items and was a sucker for brightly colored, mismatched dishes.

Her designs for clients might be clean with calm colors, but in her own life, Kristen loved the wild and unique.

"Well, at least let me give you my old dishes."

"Old? Did you buy new ones?"

Amy turned to her with a smile. "Just yesterday. They're cream with blue flowers."

Kristen thought about how much Amy loved to shop. "I think you have a problem." Kristen opened the fridge and stuck her head inside, then groaned when she saw that it was completely empty. "Maybe I need to stage an intervention to curb your habit."

Amy laughed. "No, what I need is a man."

Kristen peeked over at her. "I'm off of those for a while. Maybe I'll take up shopping instead."

"Right." Amy shook her head at her. "I give you two weeks."

"Two weeks for what?"

"Two weeks until you call me up and tell me that you've found 'the one.'" Her friend made air quotes.

"Can I help it if I fall in love easily?"

"Yes, yes, you can."

"I'm hungry," she said, changing the subject. "We didn't get any food. What do you say to buying me some tacos?"

Amy laughed at her for changing the subject and then smiled. "Tacos, it is. And I think a margarita is in order as well."

◆　◆　◆

It took Kristen precisely three weeks to get over Rod. That's when she'd bumped into Christian, and she'd quickly forgotten all about her troubles over the last month. When she'd seen his blue eyes and his smile, she'd simply melted.

He'd been a complete gentleman and had let her cut in line at Starbucks after she'd almost knocked him over. His hand had rested on hers, and she'd felt her heart skip.

Their first date—if you could call it that—had been the very next day at the same spot. He'd bought her coffee and a muffin and they had sat in the back booth talking. He was a lawyer of some type, working for a firm downtown. She didn't really get much information since he didn't like to talk about himself.

Instead, he'd asked her question after question and had seemed really interested in her life. He listened intently and she had just gotten more lost in those blue eyes of his and rambled on.

When he'd asked her to meet him again, the next day, same time, same place, she hadn't even blinked an eye. She'd rushed out after work that night and had bought herself a new outfit to wear the following day.

Their relationship continued to grow in the coffee shop over the next week, and when he finally asked her to dinner, she was both nervous and excited.

"I really think this is the one," she told Amy over the phone as she finished putting on her makeup.

"Well, he's a step up from an unemployed auto mechanic."

"I just liked Rod for his body." She smiled, remembering how sexy all his tattoos and muscles had been.

"And look at where that got you," Amy said dryly. "Does that mean this man is an overweight middle-aged guy?"

"No, just the opposite. Think Ryan Gosling in *The Notebook*." She sighed dreamily again, thinking about it.

"Uh-oh," Amy said.

"What?"

"Nothing." The line was silent for a while.

"No, what does 'uh-oh' mean?" She set down her brush and stared at her reflection. She loved the way her new teal shirt looked with the flowing cream-colored skirt she wore.

She'd left her caramel hair down, letting her curls fall naturally around her face.

"It just means that you've done it again."

"What?" She frowned at her reflection.

"Fallen for the same type of guy."

"Uh, hello. He's a lawyer. I've never fallen for a lawyer before. You can't go wrong with a name like Christian Bower the Second. He has a number at the end of his name." She almost squealed the last part.

"Just wait, just watch. Something will happen. He'll end up being a janitor at a law firm or . . ." She groaned a little. "Worse, he'll steal your personal information and max out all your credit cards."

Kristen laughed. "I do have bad luck with men, but the bad streak is over. I can just tell."

"Honey, you have more than just bad luck with men; you have bad luck period. Or did you forget—"

"Don't." She held up her hand and closed her eyes to the truth.

"I'm just saying . . ."

"I know," she moaned. "But since there is no way to reverse what that witch did . . ."

"There are no such things as witches. Well, except for Wiccans, but they don't have magical powers."

"This one did."

She cringed when she remembered what had happened last year. Then she looked down at her watch and gasped. "I've got to go. I'm meeting him in half an hour."

"Meeting? He's not picking you up?"

"No. I thought it would be best to not have to explain why I don't have furniture." She looked around her still-empty apartment.

"Fine, but call me the second you get home."

"Yes, Mother." She smirked. "Wish me luck."

"You're going to need more than that." Amy added, "But good luck and have fun."

CHAPTER TWO

That night was one of the best nights she could remember. Christian had taken her to Ruth's Chris Steak House. She'd passed by the place for years but had never stepped inside due to the prices on the menu that hung outside.

The food was fantastic, the atmosphere perfect, and her date had been dashing. As they were walking out, he hinted at going back to her place, but she demurred.

"I'm having the place redecorated." She silently hoped he'd invite her to his place, but he just smiled and nodded. He walked her back to the light rail stop and waited for the next tram. Then he pulled her into the darkness of the stop and kissed her until she felt her toes curl.

When she walked into her apartment less than half an hour later, she called Amy and told her friend everything.

"That settles it. We need to hit the furniture store this weekend." Kristen sighed and rested her phone on her shoulder. "Do you think we can borrow your brother's truck?"

"I'll message him in the morning. Have you gotten the check from your insurance company yet?" Amy asked.

"No, but they told me it should be coming any day. I just hope it's enough to get something decent."

"Anything is a step up from the blue thing you called a sofa last time," Amy added.

"Betty had character." Kristen defended the old sofa that she had loved from the moment she'd gotten it.

"And fleas," Amy added. Her friend sounded like she was holding back her laughter.

"No, she didn't. You just didn't like that she was a classic." Kristen felt like she had to defend the old sofa, which, to be perfectly honest, had been a bad choice.

"Honey, you're an interior designer. Why you choose the furniture you do for yourself is beyond me. I've seen some of the places you've designed, all pieces of art. The rooms you did for the old hotel downtown were simply amazing. Why you don't use that talent for your own place is the real question."

"Those are clients." She frowned and tried to get comfortable on the air mattress. "Besides, just because I have unique personal taste doesn't mean that the pieces I pick out for myself aren't nice. Do you remember my dining room table?"

"Yes, that's the only piece I truly miss." Her friend sighed. "Well, I have an early morning. I'm trying to sell the place up in Breckenridge, which means a long drive tomorrow."

Amy had been working at Rocky Mountain Real Estate as a realtor for the past few years after interning at the business all throughout college. Amy had told Kristen she'd be made for the job and Kristen believed her. Her friend had never been happier going to work.

"Be safe. I hear we're in for some more snow."

"Yeah, I'd heard. It's a good thing I haven't had my snow tires switched out yet."

"Call me when you get home."

"Yes, Mom." Amy chuckled.

"Night."

Kristen lay there in the dark and reviewed the evening in her head. Building up relationships was something she was good at. Turning little glances into steamy looks, small kisses into passionate ones.

Still, as she fell asleep, she dreamed of the perfect man and slept like a baby on the most uncomfortable bed she'd ever had.

The week flew by. Almost every day, she ran into Christian at the coffee shop. Some days he was in a hurry or she was and they only had time to chat for a minute or two.

She had hoped that he'd ask her out again, but he had mentioned that he would be out of town over the weekend for business.

When Saturday came along, she was thrilled when Amy showed up with her brother's truck.

"I have never gone to just one store to shop for furniture before," she warned as Amy parked the truck in front of the large warehouse building.

"Home Time Furniture is an okay place to buy standard stuff. I figured we'd start here first, since they have, like, a zillion sofas."

Amy pocketed her brother's keys and took Kristen's arm as they walked into the store together. "If we don't find something here, we can move on. So, I'm thinking you should go with leather."

Kristen's eyebrows shot up. "I'm not sure. I don't like to feel sticky during the summer and cold in the winter."

"Some of the new leather is so soft, you'll overlook the temperature issue."

"I'm open-minded." She was telling the truth. She really was trying to keep an open mind. After all, this is what she did for a living. She'd picked out leather for multiple clients before, and every one of them had been completely happy with her choices.

"I had forgotten how huge this place is. How are we ever going to find just one sofa I like?" She looked around. "I think it's easier to pick things out for my clients."

"There's even a second floor." Her friend pointed toward the large stairs that sat in the middle of the room. "I bought my dresser here last year. It took me almost three hours to find the one I wanted. This place is amazing." Amy was looking around like she had plenty of energy to spare.

Kristen knew that they would be there for hours and glanced down at her feet. "I wish I had my old UGGs." She frowned at her new pair and wiggled her toes. They weren't as comfortable as her old ones, even though she had to silently admit they looked a whole lot nicer.

"Let's start down here and make our way across the room." Amy tugged on her hand until she followed her.

An hour later, she plopped down on a sofa that looked like the one, but it was hard as stone and so uncomfortable, she immediately jumped up.

She'd lost Amy almost five minutes earlier. One minute her friend had been standing beside her, the next she'd been gone. So, Kristen had walked around calling out her name like a lost child until she'd gotten distracted by the sofa. The most perfect sofa she'd ever seen.

She glared down at the thing in disgust. How could something so good-looking be so uncomfortable? When she started to back away from the hardest sofa she'd ever sat on, she bumped solidly into someone and almost fell over.

Strong hands went up to her shoulders as she turned around and gasped.

Christian stood there looking at her like she'd just punched him in the gut.

"Oh." She smiled and reached out to put her arms around him, but he quickly dropped his hands and took a huge step backward. "Fancy running into you."

He nodded and looked around quickly.

Instantly Kristen could tell that something was wrong. "I thought you were . . ."

"Christian, what do you think about this one?" asked a tall, slender blonde woman, who was holding a little blond boy in her arms as a little girl about three years old followed her. The woman walked over and looked down at the sofa Kristen had just vacated.

Kristen's heart bumped in her chest as Christian watched the woman sit down on the hard sofa. The little girl climbed up beside her.

"That one's nice," he mumbled, then looked at Kristen.

She took a giant step back and almost knocked over a lamp on an end table. The woman's gaze locked on her and she smiled slightly. Then Kristen looked, really looked, from the three people sitting on the sofa to Christian and knew.

"There you are," Amy said behind her.

Kristen turned quickly and grabbed her friend's hand and pulled her away.

"What?" Amy glanced over her shoulder. "What's wrong?"

Kristen shook her head and continued to tug on her friend, knowing the tears would be falling soon. She didn't look back; she couldn't.

Finally, after getting lost in the huge place, she pulled to a stop in a small alcove area and sat down on a large bed and closed her eyes.

"That was Mr. Wonderful, wasn't it?" Amy said, sitting next to her and putting her arm around Kristen's shoulders.

Kristen nodded and felt the tears sting her eyes.

"I'm sorry," Amy said quietly.

She shook her head quickly from side to side. "I should have guessed."

"How? How could you have known that he had a family?"

She shrugged and looked at her friend. "The curse."

Amy tilted her head. "Let's get out of here and grab some lunch. I no longer feel like shopping here."

Kristen stood quickly and prayed that they would make it out of the store without bumping into Mr. and Mrs. Christian Bower II and family.

◆ ◆ ◆

"What do you mean you bought a new car?" Amy sounded anxious over the phone.

Kristen smiled at herself in her new rearview mirror. "I bought a car. My insurance check came, and since I wasn't in the mood to go furniture shopping again"—she frowned, remembering the shock of three weeks ago—"I decided to treat myself instead."

"What did you do?" She heard Amy sigh.

"I used my insurance check as a down payment on a brand-new cherry-red Ford Mustang convertible." She felt the machine purr underneath her. "We're on our way to you now so you can drool over her and I can take you for a spin."

"Kristen." She heard the warning in her friend's voice. "Are you sure . . ."

"Never been surer." She relaxed back and felt the rich leather of the steering wheel in her hands. "Leather interior. You did say I needed leather, didn't you?" She giggled.

"I'm happy for you, if this is really what you want."

"It is. Just think of it. This way, I can drive out to see you and my folks more often. I have always hated riding the bus from Denver to Golden," she said as she stopped at a red light. She wished it weren't drizzling so she could put the top down. Maybe the sun would come out tomorrow and she could go for a long ride.

She heard a knock on the window and jumped a little. Then her door was yanked open and a gun was pointed directly in her face.

"Out! Now!" the man screamed at her.

Her eyes locked on the end of the gun. If he hadn't reached in and yanked her out of the car, she would have sat there frozen with fear.

When her hands and knees hit the cement, she jolted free from the frozen shock she'd been in. She turned and watched her new red Mustang peel out as she sat on the side of the road.

"Kristen!" she heard in the earbud in her ear.

She jolted and fumbled for her cell phone in her jacket pocket.

"I . . . I just got carjacked," she said, feeling her head spin.

"Are you okay? Where are you? I'm calling the police."

Fifteen minutes later, Kristen sat in the back of a police car and relayed the entire story. She felt like a fool that she couldn't remember even one detail about the man who had stolen her car, her purse, and her dignity.

Amy showed up with her brother, who asked more questions than the police had.

They drove her out to Amy's place in Golden and sat with her while she called her insurance company and explained how the car they had just started insuring that morning had been stolen.

Since she had been talked into starting the dealer's antitheft protection plan, the police had assured her that it wouldn't take long to track the car down. Ten minutes after the police had called, the dealer activated the GPS. They hadn't given her any more information but had assured her that they would call her once they recovered her new ride.

She hated to admit it, but just like shopping for furniture, buying a car was tainted now for her as well, and she thought about selling the flashy car as soon as she got it back.

What had she been thinking? Buying a car? She hated driving. Hated car payments. Hated that she'd been so stupid as to not think about her curse.

She rested her head on Amy's table, feeling completely and utterly defeated.

"Honey, it's not your fault." Amy rubbed a hand over her back.

"Yeah, it is. I should have known."

"I'm just thankful that you're okay. Last month a man was shot downtown in a carjacking."

She felt her skin grow cold as she glanced up at Amy. "I'm never driving again."

"Come on, I'll drive you home."

"You're smart," she said as her friend helped her walk outside with a hand in hers. "You drive that." She nodded at Amy's sensible car, which was parked in front of her condo. "You'd never do anything as dumb as buy a flashy sports car. Though, it did feel wonderful to drive."

"The police will recover it. I bet they already have it. It was smart to get the protection."

"It doesn't matter," she croaked as she sank into her friend's worn seats. "It's ruined like everything else."

"Don't say that." Amy glanced at her as she pulled out of the parking spot.

"Why? Do you honestly think that I would feel safe driving that thing again? Every time I'm stopped at a stop sign I'll have a panic attack." She tried not to hyperventilate now just thinking about it.

When her cell phone rang, she answered it quickly.

"Miss Collins? This is Detective Hopkins with the Lakewood police."

"Yes?" She held her breath.

"We've located your vehicle." She could hear the pause and knew it was bad. "Unfortunately, it appears that the thief lost control of the vehicle. The car was found upside down in Bear Creek just outside of Morrison. We're having the car towed and should have a final report sent over to your insurance company in the next few weeks."

She felt frustration consume her and closed her eyes. At least she wouldn't have to try and sell the car now.

"Is it totaled?"

"I'm afraid so, ma'am. With the recent weather we've had, the water in the creek was pretty high, and the car was slammed into some rocks."

"Did . . ." She swallowed. "Did the man who stole it . . . ?"

"He jumped from the car before it hit the water. We have him in custody. He's bruised up some but alive."

"My purse? My things?"

"Sorry, ma'am. It looks like most of what was in the car floated away in the water. We'll keep an eye out for it as we pull your car out of the water, but so far, we haven't recovered any of your belongings. If I was you, I'd still cancel all your cards, just in case."

"Thank you." She rubbed her hand over her temple and desperately wished for some aspirin.

She hung up and then opened her eyes to see Amy holding a bottle of pills in front of her. "I don't have any water, but we can stop somewhere and get some lunch so you can take some of these." She shook the bottle of Tylenol. Kristen choked, "It's gone." Then chuckled at the ironic joke her life was. It was worse than an Alanis Morissette song. Feeling her stomach turn, she took a drink of the water. "Upside down in a river."

"Oh!" Amy reached over and took her hand. "I'm sorry, sweetie."

She shook her head. "Don't be. It's better this way."

Amy pulled her car into a fast food restaurant parking lot and then turned to her. "Promise me one thing."

She turned to her friend. "Anything."

"This time, when the insurance cuts you a check, let me know before you do anything drastic again."

She accepted her fate and nodded her head quickly. "You've got it. I am never jumping into anything ever again."

CHAPTER
THREE

Aiden Scott wasn't the type of man who jumped into anything. He prided himself on weighing risk versus gain in every situation in life. Years of running his own business had taught him that lesson, but years of dating women who knew how to get what they wanted had honed his tendency toward caution.

So, when he was asked by two of his stepfather's best friends to look into buying out their company, he wanted to know everything he could about the business.

Row and Stein Architecture Firm had been in business for over thirty years. Steven Row was one of his stepfather's best friends from college. The man had practically lived with his stepfather the first few years after he'd started his business. Actually, it was Steven Row who had initially gotten Aiden interested in the development field.

Aiden's stepfather, Eric, had introduced Steven to Paul Stein, who bought into the small firm several years later and turned the business into what it was today.

One of the top architecture firms in Denver, they not only restored a lot of the older buildings downtown but also designed some of the newer office buildings and lofts that were popping up around the metro area.

Aiden had been very surprised when Eric had asked him to sit down with Paul and Steven to discuss the possibilities of a business deal where he would absorb the successful business into his own.

"I'd like to spend some time at your offices," he said as their meeting in his own building wound down.

"Um, sure," the older, silver-haired man agreed. "Anytime. You're always welcome."

"I'd need some office space, and I'd like to look over your books."

"That's Paul's area." He gestured to his business partner.

"I'll make the arrangements." The heavier man nodded.

"Good. I've got a few things to tie up here first. I can start in two weeks."

The men glanced at each other. "How soon could you make a decision?"

"In a hurry?" He frowned.

They both shook their heads. "No, not at all. It's just we have a few big projects coming up and . . ." Paul sighed. "We were sure hoping for some extra help."

Aiden replied, "Once I get my foot in the door, it should take me only a few weeks, maybe a month, to make up my mind." He thought about his schedule and rearranged a few things in his head.

"Good." Steven smiled at him. "I knew talking to Eric about bringing you in was a great idea.

"Let's clear something up. I'm not looking to become partner. If I do this, I'll buy the both of you out. If you want to stay on, I'll respect that and add it to the contracts, but if I decide to step in, it will be a full takeover. I'll absorb Row and Stein completely."

The men nodded in agreement and their smiles grew. "We've both decided that we're too old and tired to continue running things like we've been doing. Neither of our kids wanted to follow in our footsteps, so we can't hand the business down to family. Shame my son turned out to be a surgeon," he said.

Aiden smiled. "From what Eric tells me, a pretty good one too."

Steven's smile was bigger now. "Damn good."

"I'll make those arrangements and have all the paperwork ready when you arrive," Paul said. "Oh, one more thing." Paul glanced at Steven quickly. "We want to keep this under the radar for now. No one can know about it outside us and the board members. Not until we've agreed to a deal."

Aiden shook both of the men's hands and watched the men leave. It was easy enough for him to read between the lines and know that they were having difficulty dealing with their growth and handling the financial responsibilities that came with success.

Aiden had been using Row and Stein Architects for the last five years for his own business and knew that the firm provided quality. In the years he'd used them, he'd never had any problems and had always enjoyed working with them.

But since Urban Development was Aiden's baby, he didn't want to jump into anything quickly. Not when it could jeopardize his business. He loved being a developer, but he loved being a business owner even more.

He could use a slight distraction. He was in between relationships and had plenty of time to focus on work, which was kind of slowly driving him crazy. This was just what he needed right now.

"Lisa?" He stepped out of his office and waited for his secretary to follow him back in. He walked around and sat behind his desk. "I'll need to move my schedule around."

◆ ◆ ◆

Two weeks later, Aiden walked toward the silver thirty-story building downtown that housed the offices of Row and Stein Architecture Firm.

He'd been in the high-rise building on several occasions but had never been to the seventh level where the firm consumed the entire floor.

As he walked toward the rotating doors out front, he was bumped into from behind and almost knocked to the ground by a hurricane.

The first thing he noticed was the mass of hair flying in the heavy wind. High winds were common in downtown Denver, and today was no exception. He had struggled to keep his tie tucked in his jacket as he'd stepped off the bus into the wind earlier. So when the woman bumped solidly into him, he held on to her, assuming that her hair had blocked her sight and she just hadn't seen him.

Her long green skirt was flying around, and even though the thing reached her ankles, she held on to it with a death grip to keep it from rising above her head.

There was a stack of papers tucked under her arm, as well as a large black tube for holding designs.

When she had knocked into him, some of her papers had flown out of her hands. She reached out to grab them and lost hold of her skirt, which rushed up high on her thighs. He was rewarded with a view of the sexiest pair of legs he'd ever seen.

It took him a moment to stop staring at the perfect, silky legs and spring into action. He reached out and grabbed at the papers that were flying around their heads in a whirlwind.

Finally, when he'd snagged the last paper from the air, he turned to her and stopped dead. He'd thought the legs were perfect. The rest of her was even better.

Her green eyes laughed at him as she tried to hold her skirt to her body and tame her long hair at the same time.

"I thought they were going to end up in Kansas, and then my next meeting would have been shot to hell." She laughed. "Thank you." She took the papers from him.

He stood there like a fool. He probably even had his mouth open, but he was too distracted to notice. All he knew was that his heart tried to escape his chest as the woman quickly walked away from him and into the building.

It took him a few seconds to react and he tried to follow her, but when he entered the building, she was nowhere to be seen.

He shook off his disappointment and made his way to the mirrored elevators. When he finally walked into the Row and Stein's offices, he was impressed.

The cream-colored carpet accented the warm wood walls in the entryway. A shiny metal sign hung on a wall made with refurbished wood and reused bricks and stone. The mixture of new and old didn't go unnoticed.

He was greeted by a blonde woman who sat behind the high receptionist desk. "Welcome to Row and Stein Architecture. Can I help you?"

"Aiden Scott to see Mr. Row and Mr. Stein."

She nodded, then picked up her phone. A few moments later, she smiled up at him. "Mr. Row and Mr. Stein will see you now, Mr. Scott." She motioned for him to follow her.

He walked through a massive room filled with people sitting behind large-screen computers and drafting desks. He noticed a long conference room that looked much like the one in his office.

"Mr. Row, Mr. Scott is here." The woman stepped aside and Steven stood up from behind a very messy desk.

"There you are, my boy." Steven walked over and shook his hand and slapped him on the shoulder.

"Thanks, Shirley. Let's go into Paul's office; he's the neat and tidy one." He walked across the room toward another row of offices along the windows. "When my boys were little, I once lost them in that mess." He pointed back toward his office and laughed. "Here's our savior now," he said, leaning into Paul's office.

Paul Stein's office looked a lot like his own did. Tidy and organized. There was a large drafting table and two massive screens that showed the man was currently working on designs for something big.

"Oh good. I've got a place all set up for you." Paul stood and shook his hand. "I'll show you to it. Everything should be ready."

They walked a few offices down and Aiden was shown into an office roughly the same size as the other two. This one was cleared of everything except two large computer screens.

"The IT guy, Darren, should be around soon to show you how to get on the network and set up your user info. That file cabinet has most of our financial information in it. The rest is up on the network that Darren will give you access to."

"I've arranged for you to go out on a couple different jobs, if you want, with some of our people," Steven said, leaning against the doorjamb.

"I appreciate it. I'll spend a few days looking over this and then let you know."

"As far as it goes around here"—Steven leaned in and shut the door behind him—"we haven't mentioned the possibility of being bought out to any of the employees yet. They think you're here for a trial period as a new employee."

"We'd kind of like to keep it that way until we get your final answer," Paul added.

Aiden nodded. "I'll let you know when I've made a decision."

"If you need anything, just let us know," Paul said just as Steven opened the door to a dark-haired man in khakis and a black button-up shirt.

"Here's Darren now to set you up."

The two partners left and Aiden spent the next half hour learning their network. By the time Darren left, Aiden had to admit that his own IT guy was failing on the job; Urban Developers' network wasn't as efficient as this one was. Nor was his IT personnel as well informed.

He spent the next two hours glued to the screen, looking over the business's spreadsheets for the last two years. Whoever did the books did a fine job. Everything was well organized and he had an easy time finding everything.

Lunchtime rolled around and Steven knocked on the door and asked if he'd like to join them for lunch. He followed the men down to the lobby and they ate at the well-known sushi place on the main floor. He enjoyed the two men's conversation during lunch and realized just how close the older men were, which only had him thinking about his own relationships again.

As they rode the elevators back up to the seventh floor, he received a message to call his office. He excused himself so he could go back into his new office area to return the call.

When he walked in, the caramel-haired beauty from before sat with her feet propped up on his desk as she sucked down a long strand of ramen noodles.

When she noticed him, she started coughing on the noodles she'd just inhaled. He rushed over and began patting her on the back.

◆　◆　◆

She couldn't believe her luck. Her bad luck. The man she'd almost knocked down was standing outside her lunch area. Well, the empty office she'd used as her private lunch area for the last year and a half.

His dark hair, which had gotten messed up by the wind, had been combed down and slicked back. His suit was perfectly in place and he had the most annoyed look on his face, like he'd had when he'd first looked at her.

His hand continued to pound her back, even after she'd gotten air back in her lungs.

"I'm okay now," she said between slaps on the back.

"You sure?" He stopped, his hand in midair.

She nodded and swallowed.

"What are you doing here?" He looked down at her and she couldn't really read what he was thinking in his dark eyes.

"I . . ." She blinked a few times. "I work here. What are you doing here?" She set her chopsticks down and glared at him.

"I . . ." He shut his mouth quickly. "I work here too."

"Noooo." She thought about it—she knew they hadn't hired anyone in the last few months. After all, she'd been told there was a hiring freeze in place. "You don't. I know everyone that works here, and I know for a fact that we haven't hired anyone new lately."

He just looked down at her with those dark eyes and a slight frown on his lips. "I've answered your question, now it's your turn."

She shook her head. "You've avoided my question." She moved to get up to go find Paul to get more information.

"No, I told you. I work here." He held out his hand. "Aiden Scott."

She looked at his hand and wondered why she didn't believe or trust the man. "Kristen Collins."

His eyebrows shot up as he asked, "Interior designer?"

She nodded and crossed her arms over her chest, avoiding shaking his hand. She watched him drop his arm to his side.

"Well, Miss Collins, you're sitting in my new office." He motioned. "And I'd like to get back to work."

She balked. "They gave you the big office?"

He looked around. "Big? It's the same size as Steven's and Paul's."

"You're calling them by their first names." No one called their bosses by their first names, except her, since she'd known them her entire life.

He nodded. "Friends of the family." His eyebrows went up, no doubt waiting for more questions.

Gathering her lunch, she moved to get out of the chair, only to have the thing slide too fast and bump into the table behind her. Her skirt caught under the wheel and she heard a loud rip.

Closing her eyes, she cringed. "There goes my new skirt." She should have known better than to wear a flowing skirt after hearing the high-wind warning that morning on the news.

She thought she heard a chuckle, but when she looked up at the man, his eyes were on her skirt. Looking down, she saw that not only had it torn, but it had torn down the entire front seam. Half of her thigh was now exposed.

"Ruined," she surmised. "That will teach me to splurge." She stood up and continued to look down at her skirt. It was a shame; she had really liked the soft material. And the color had matched her eyes perfectly. Maybe she could sew it back together. What was she thinking? The last time she'd tried to sew anything, she'd ended up with so many holes in her thumb that she'd given up trying. "Well, it was nice to meet you." She glanced up at him, but when she noticed that his eyes were still on her skirt, she grabbed up her lunch and rushed out.

Now she would have to either find some other place to eat lunch every day or—she cringed again—eat at her own desk. Which never worked since everyone could find her and she would end up working through the half hour.

The second she sat back down at her desk, Roger walked up and handed her another assignment.

She sighed and set her bowl of noodles aside, knowing they would be cold before she could get back to them.

She made a mental note to ask Paul what was up with the new guy. Aiden Scott. Why did that name sound so familiar to her?

She shook her head clear and tried to concentrate on her work.

Just before five, her coworker Carla walked over and handed her an envelope. "Here's your ticket for this week." Kristen was in a weekly lotto pool. Some weeks it was scratch tickets, others state lotto tickets. She knew she didn't have a chance of winning, but she'd signed up the month she'd been hired at R&S and hadn't had the heart to tell Carla she no longer had the good luck to win anything.

"Thanks." Kristen stuffed the envelope in her jacket pocket.

"Did you see Mr. Dreamy?" Carla patted the spot over her heart and rolled her eyes as she sat on the edge of Kristen's desk.

"Hmm?" She turned and glanced at the woman. She was tall, skinny, and looked like she'd stepped off the cover of a magazine. Her beauty was one of the main reasons she'd been hired, according to the rumors that were spreading around the office.

"You know, Mr. Hunk in the empty office." She motioned toward the corner office. "Don't tell me you haven't noticed him," Carla whispered.

"No, I mean, yeah, I talked to him."

"You talked to him?" She gasped a little.

"Sure." She rested back and crossed her arms over her chest, mentally telling herself she needed a few more padded bras.

"About what?" Carla leaned closer and Kristen was assaulted with an accidental view of the woman's perfect breasts as her shirt flopped open a little.

Kristen blinked and avoided the flawless cleavage in her face.

"He said he works here." She averted her eyes and looked over to where Aiden's office was.

"That's it?"

"Um, and his name is Aiden Scott." Her mind spun again, trying to figure out where she'd heard his name. Just the thought of his dark eyes watching her had her skin warming.

"Hmm." Carla leaned back and Kristen was thankful when her shirt fell back into place. "Aiden. Such a sexy name."

"I guess." Kristen had thought the same thing when she'd heard it, but she kept trying to deny it to herself. She didn't like dark-haired men with sexy brown eyes that were too hard to read.

"I can't believe you didn't swoon when he talked to you."

She chuckled. "No, but I almost choked."

Carla looked at her in question.

"He surprised me while I was eating lunch." She nodded to her still-full bowl of noodles. "I almost choked on my noodles, but he slapped my back until I could breathe again."

"I would have died." Carla sighed. "A man like him, saving my life." She sighed again, louder this time.

Kristen almost rolled her eyes. Aiden had *not* saved her life. "I guess Aiden Scott just isn't my type," she said, hoping that Carla would get the hint. Then she heard someone clear his throat.

When she glanced over, she could feel her face turn beet red. She froze, locking onto his dark brown eyes.

Carla chose that moment to rush from her cubicle as fast as her long legs would carry her.

"That's a shame. Just what is your type?" He leaned on the half wall of her cubicle like he wasn't going anywhere soon.

She swallowed and prayed that her face wasn't as red as it felt.

"I'm sure I don't know what you're talking about." She tried to turn back toward her computer, but he rested his hand on her armrest to keep her facing him.

"You just told that woman that I'm not your type."

"Carla," she corrected and watched him nod.

"You just told Carla that I'm not your type. I'd like to know what your type consists of." His smile grew and she noticed that his eyes were a lighter shade of brown than she had thought.

She shrugged, keeping her eyes locked with his. "Well, if my track record stands, my next boyfriend will either be a terrorist or an international jewel thief."

He blinked a few times and then laughed, and for the first time in her twenty-three years, she found herself attracted to a dark-haired, brown-eyed man. She was completely thrown off.

CHAPTER
FOUR

Aiden couldn't explain why he was drawn to the beauty. He'd over-heard her tell the blonde that he wasn't her type. Well, the same could be said for him.

Actually, the busty blonde who had quickly vacated Kristen's cubi-cle was more of his type. She looked almost exactly like his last three girlfriends.

But his eyes had locked on the honey-haired, green-eyed beauty with the sexy legs. He glanced down and noticed that her skirt had fallen open so he could see her exposed thigh. His mouth went dry just looking at it, looking at her.

"Paul tells me that I'll be working with you on the Market Place job." He leaned in a little, making sure to keep his hand on her chair.

He watched her dark eyebrows go up slowly in question.

"Paul and Steven want me to go out on a couple jobs. You know, to get my feet wet."

She nodded slightly, but he could tell there were a million questions running around in her head.

"Go ahead, check my story." He smiled, liking the fact that she didn't take everything at face value.

Since meeting her at lunch, he'd spent the last three hours looking at her personnel file, along with everything she'd ever done for the business. He was more than impressed. He was totally turned on.

Not only did the woman seem to know her job, but her work was neat, tidy, and she was extremely talented. Not to mention sexy as hell.

He mentally shook his head and watched as she shoved a mass of those curls behind her ear. She was wearing long silver earrings with small little balls at the ends. She wore several different rings on her long fingers and he had a sudden urge to put those digits one by one into his mouth and suck until . . .

"There's no need. I spoke with Paul myself." When she used Paul's first name, he looked at her in question.

"Using his first name?" he asked and saw the irritation cross her eyes.

"I grew up living near him." She tried to turn her chair away from him, but he held it still as he smiled down at her.

"Did you go to school with his son, Jeff?"

She nodded, and this time it was she that looked at him in question. "You?"

He shook his head and left it at that.

He grinned when irritation crossed her eyes, turning them a deeper green.

"Interesting," he mumbled.

"What is?" She crossed her arms over her chest, causing her breasts to push up a bit more out of her shirt. His eyes zeroed in on the move. "Your eyes." He looked back at those green globes and watched them darken even more.

She sighed. "Mr. Scott, if you don't mind, I have three more hours of work ahead of me." She glanced down at his hand.

"Let me know when you plan on going out to the Market Place job again. I'll tag along."

"I'll keep you posted. Until then, you can study up on my drawings. They're under the folder—"

"I've seen them," he broke in, earning another irritated look from her.

"Fine," she said, and then she turned around and started typing on her keyboard.

He walked back to his office and closed down the machine for the day. On his way out, he stopped and talked to both Steven and Paul. Paul presented him with a set of keys and the code to get into the building after hours.

"The building security has your information and shouldn't bother you if you need to work at night." He motioned. "Sometimes Darren is here, running backups or fixing downed machines. Just let him know if you need anything."

He nodded. "Damn, I might have to steal that man from you." He thought about his own team and knew there was room for improvement. "Our own IT crews leave at five sharp and we're lucky to get anything done during business hours."

"Absorb us and he's all yours." He laughed and slapped him on the back.

"I guess that's as good a motivation as any." When he walked out, he glanced over and saw the top of Kristen's head at her desk and wondered how long she worked.

She'd mentioned that she had a few more hours ahead of her.

He had a few hours of his own work piled up at his office. He knew it was going to mean some serious overtime if he was going to get his work for both his company and R&S done. But he was up for the challenge.

When he got to his office, after riding the bus down Sixteenth Street, he couldn't help but notice the differences between the two buildings.

He'd purchased the old stone place four years ago and had spent a year renovating it. There was state-of-the-art everything, yet he'd made sure to keep the classic charms of the older building. The stone and brick walls that ran through the place made it feel like a second home to him.

All the larger offices were on the second floor, where most of the designers and developers worked. On the main level were the meeting rooms, file storage, and all of the servers and computer equipment. There was also a small lunch area and break room for the staff.

The place was plenty big enough for double the number of employees that were currently housed in it. He was beginning to see that his plan was feasible. Leaning back in his chair, he let his mind wander to the staff at R&S. He kept finding it harder to avoid having Kristen's image pop into his mind as he worked. He kept playing over their first meeting and caught himself chuckling several times instead of working. Shaking his head clear, he tried harder to stay focused on the task at hand.

Around seven that night, he shut down his computer and hopped on the bus back to his condo. As he rode the elevator up to the twenty-fifth floor, he thought about Kristen once more and wondered if she was still sitting in her tiny cubicle. If her skirt was still showing that sexy leg. He sighed and remembered how her legs had looked.

Maybe he needed to get out a little more. After all, in the last six months he'd been so busy with jobs that he hadn't taken any time for himself.

All he needed was a hot date.

But every time he thought about calling one of the women from his past, a green-eyed, honey-haired beauty with damn sexy legs kept popping up in his head.

◆ ◆ ◆

Kristen pulled her jacket around herself tightly and wished more than anything that she hadn't missed the earlier train. When she'd left her apartment, the sun had been out and it actually looked like the weather was going to contradict the weatherman by staying sunny and warm.

But she'd spent so much time enjoying her short walk to the train station that she'd missed the early train. By the time the next one pulled up, the sky had darkened and the wind had kicked in, making her wish she'd grabbed her heavier jacket.

She glanced at her watch. How was it that on days she needed to get to the office early, she was always late? She tucked her hands into her coat and felt the envelope Carla had given her two days ago.

Might as well see what she had.

Pulling out the ticket, she dug out a coin from her purse and started scratching.

One triple seven, two triple seven. She took a deep breath and, even though she'd done it a million times, silently wished for the third triple seven. Not that she would win big bucks, just ten thousand dollars. But triple sevens was better than no sevens. She sighed and wondered how long she could avoid clearing off the last spot.

She glanced up and noticed that she was one stop from her own, and without looking, cleared the last spot. She avoided peering down at it until the train began to slow. When she did, she gasped and then stopped herself from crinkling up the card.

Triple sevens. She'd hit the jackpot of ten thousand dollars. Ten thousand dollars! She quickly grabbed her bag and purse and rushed out the open doors.

By the time she sat down at her desk, she was completely and utterly winded. She knew her hair must have looked a mess, and she probably had a wild and crazy look on her face, but she didn't care.

She quickly snatched up her phone and punched Amy's number.

"Guess what?" she squealed and then glanced around as everyone in her office looked her way.

"What? What's wrong?" Amy sounded panicked.

Kristen laughed, then leaned closer to the phone and whispered, "Nothing. For once, something wonderful has happened."

"What?" She heard excitement in her friend's voice.

"I won. I won the lottery."

"What?" This time it was Amy's voice that rose.

"I won the scratch off. Ten thousand dollars." She closed her eyes as she sent her chair spinning a little.

"Congratulations," a deep voice said from behind her.

She gasped and almost dropped the phone.

"Who is that?" Amy asked, still sounding excited.

"Uh, got to go. Call you later." She hung up the phone quickly.

"Sounds like a celebration is in order. What do you say to lunch?" Aiden leaned on her desk.

"Um." She glanced around and noticed that everyone within hearing distance was staring, waiting for her answer.

"I'd love to see the winning ticket." His dark eyebrows shot up.

She nodded, not really paying attention, then reached inside her coat pocket and came up short. Frantically, she searched the other pocket. Then she rushed over and dumped out her purse.

"Problem?" He frowned down at her as she felt herself start to hyperventilate.

"No, it was . . . I put it . . ." She mentally retraced her steps. "I left it on the train." It came out as a whisper.

"You left the winning ticket? On the train?" He blinked a few times.

"That witch," she growled under her breath.

"Who? Someone on the train? Did they steal it from you?" He looked instantly concerned and he took her shoulders gently.

She shook her head. She felt tears build up behind her eyes, so she sat back down in her chair as she rested her head on her desk.

"No, the one that cursed me," she burst out, not wanting to go into all the details.

"I guess I'm not following you."

She turned and glared at him. "You wouldn't understand."

"I'd like to. How about that lunch? You can tell me all about it."

"I'm not in the mood. Besides, I have a meeting," she lied. She felt like resting her head on her desk all day and crying.

"Well, maybe a rain check. Sorry about the ticket." He stood up and walked away. When she glanced around the room this time, everyone around her looked away quickly. It was probably clear that she wasn't in the mood to talk. She was thankful that they chose to ignore her.

Picking up her purse, she shoved everything back into it and took her cell phone out to the back balcony, the only place on the floor where the reception was good. The balcony was where the smokers usually went during break, but she was thankful it was empty at the moment. She called Amy and told her the story as she fought back the tears.

"I'm sorry, sweetie." Her friend sounded really sorry. "I just don't know what to say. I wish I was there to give you a big hug."

She nodded and felt a tear slide down her face. "It's stupid. It's not like I didn't expect something like this to happen, not after how things have been going for me." She rested on the railing and looked out over the traffic below.

"Would you stop? Self-pity is so unbecoming."

She sighed. "You're right. I'd better get back inside." She'd forgotten to wear her jacket outside and her arms and hands were freezing.

"Try to have a good day, despite its beginnings."

"Thank you for talking me off the proverbial ledge."

"Anytime."

She made her way back to her desk, past all her coworkers, who glanced at her with concern. When she got to her desk, she turned and said clearly, "Yes, I left my winning ticket on the train. I'd like to move past this and have a good day anyway. Who knows? Maybe some poor single mother who is on food stamps picked it up and can now pay her rent and feed her kids." She smiled and nodded as several people glanced her way. She turned and sat down and kept telling herself that story for the next three hours.

The rest of the morning was a blur. At noon, she took her small break for lunch and heated up her noodles. She went to go to her usual lunch spot and then frowned and sidetracked to the small conference area instead. There was a full wall of windows that overlooked the office, so it wasn't really private, but at least no one bothered her while she ate.

When she walked back to her desk, there was a small basket of her favorite cookies sitting on her chair.

Pulling out the note, she read:

You may have lost your ticket, but you'll never lose me.
—A

Tears threatened her eyes again, so she shoved a whole cookie in her mouth to combat them.

"Must be some good cookies." Aiden's voice sounded right behind her.

She gasped with surprise, only to have the cookie lodge in her throat. She coughed and spewed chunks of cookie from her mouth and he slapped at her back and apologized.

CHAPTER FIVE

"Here, drink this." Aiden handed her his bottled water and watched her face turn a deeper shade of red as she tried to breathe.

Kristen swallowed a mouthful and her eyes watered as she finally got a deep breath in and out.

"Do you always sneak up on people like that?" She glared at him through teary eyes.

He sat on the edge of her desk. "I'm sorry. I thought you had seen me." He held back a smile.

She turned away from him and used a tissue to wipe her face.

"From an admirer?" He read the note and instantly wondered who A was and if he had competition. Even though she'd made it clear that she didn't currently have a boyfriend, that didn't mean there wasn't someone lined up for the job.

She snatched the note away and tucked it back in with the cookies.

"That's none of your business." She tried to turn her chair away from him, but it bumped his knees, causing it to remain facing him. She glared at his knees, but he stayed right where he was.

"I wanted to say that I was sorry you lost your ticket." He handed her a ticket. "I know it's probably not the winning one, but . . ." He shrugged. "You never know."

She looked down at the scratch ticket that he'd hastily purchased downstairs at the little bookstore.

"Thanks," she said as she kept her eyes lowered, looking at the ticket.

"When will you be going out to the Market Place job?"

She looked up at him and sighed. "Day after tomorrow. I've got a meeting with the owners of the organic grocery store."

He'd seen her designs for the inside and was more than impressed. "Don't forget, I'd like to tag along."

She nodded. "In about an hour, Kevin, another designer, is meeting with the owners of the lofts that are going in on Spear. You might want to tag along with him on that one."

"It's already set." He leaned in a little closer and enjoyed the sweet smell of the cookies mixed with the flowery smell of her perfume.

"Is there something else you want?" She rested back in her chair and he could tell that she was fighting to stop herself from crossing her arms over her chest.

He smiled. "There are lots of things that I want," he whispered so she would be the only one to hear.

He watched her eyes turn a darker shade of green and wondered what color they would be when he kissed her.

"You're not my type." She raised her chin, but he could see it was a lie.

"Yeah, so I've heard. The funny thing is . . ." He leaned closer. "You're not my type either." He ran his hand lightly over her shoulder and felt her pulse kick under his touch. Then he stood up and walked away.

◆　◆　◆

His meeting with Kevin at the Spear place went slowly. He'd asked too many questions, which had slowed down the meeting. But he wanted to be thorough. Kevin and the owners of the new lofts hadn't seemed to mind.

They wrapped the meeting up shortly after five that night and decided to swing by a pub a few doors down to finish the talks. He knew from years of running his own development business that, half the time, business was done over a pint of beer.

By the time he walked back into his condo, he had his mind made up. If he decided not to buy out Steven and Paul, he was going to try and hire Kevin and Darren for himself.

The next day he rode the bus and watched the spring snow fall. Even though it was mid-April, he knew they could easily get another month of the white stuff.

With construction in Colorado, snow could be a hindrance. Wet, heavy snow usually caused downtown to be a mess, but since this was the light powdery stuff that blew away quickly, work went on undisturbed. Even though the temperature could get cold, the workers still plowed through their jobs.

He had gone out on several more stops with other employees from R&S. The first one had been to a rebuild of an old firehouse as a diner on First Street. He didn't care too much for Mark, the R&S employee he'd gone with; he had treated Aiden like he was a newbie. He supposed it was par for the course, since everyone was being told he was a new employee instead of someone who might be their next boss.

Still, the man's attitude had won him a spot on his short list of employees who wouldn't make the transition.

Then he'd gone out again with Kevin to another job site and was even more impressed with how the man handled customers and his job.

By the time he walked back into the R&S offices, it was past six and the snow was coming down even harder than before. He used his keys and codes to get into the building. He wanted to pick up the file and drawings for his meeting tomorrow with the owners of the Market Place grocery. The office was dim, with only a couple lights on, and he knew that everyone had most likely already left for the day.

It was a shame that he was only pretending to be a new employee. He was getting a kick out of working once again rather than being the owner who had to worry about everything beyond just getting the job done. He'd started his own business because he loved to design, loved being able to see what he'd created come to life.

As he walked toward his office, he heard a soft pounding and looked over to see a half-frozen Kristen standing outside the dark doors of the balcony. She didn't have a jacket on and there was snow falling on her head and shoulders.

Instant worry flashed through his mind.

He rushed over, yanked open the door, and quickly pulled her into the warm building and straight into his arms.

"What the hell do you think you're doing?"

♦ ♦ ♦

Everyone has had a handful of awful days in their life. You know the kind. The ones where you should have listened to your instinct and stayed in bed.

This was one of those days. Kristen had stepped in a puddle on her way to the train station and had gotten her left boot soaking wet. She'd lost or forgotten her left glove, forcing her to tuck her hand in her coat pocket the entire walk from the station to work. This had caused her bag to slip and fall off her shoulder, spilling her important paperwork in the gutter, which was filled with melting snow.

By the time she made it into work, her hair was soaked, her left foot and hand were freezing, and her nose was running.

She didn't need the chance of feeling off for her big meeting tomorrow. The rest of the day didn't go any better. Bob had called with some minor changes they wanted to make for the grocery store. Minor on his end but major on hers. She'd spent the afternoon making the changes so they would be ready for the meeting first thing in the morning.

She'd lost track of time, and when her cell phone rang, she almost didn't answer it.

"Hello?" She heard a bunch of static and quickly walked toward the back deck area, where she knew her phone reception was best. "Hello?"

"Hey, Kristy." She heard Rod's voice slur a little. "It's me, Rod."

She stepped out on the deck and felt anger shoot through her. "What do you want? To come back and finish the job by stealing the clothes off my back?"

"Naw, I just wanted to say that I'm sorry." She heard a burst of laughter in the background of his phone and felt her anger grow.

"If you're really sorry, you'll return all my things. Better yet, tell me where you are so I can tell the police." She knew that the police hadn't tracked him down because, as it turned out, he'd given her a fake last name.

He snarled. "Can't return the stuff. I hocked it."

"You what?" She almost screamed it.

"Had to. I had people to pay off. But it didn't even make a dent in my debt."

She rubbed her forehead and was slightly shocked when she realized for the first time that it was snowing. "Why did you call? Short on cash, again? Because if you think I'm going to fall for your tricks . . ." She felt chilled to the bone.

"I was hoping we could be friends, you know. We had something good between us."

"When hell freezes over!" she exclaimed. Turning around, she walked over to the outer doors and yanked on one, only to come up short. Panic spread through her as she tried the other handle.

"Jeez, you don't have to be a bitch---"

Kristen didn't even wait for him to finish talking. She punched the End button on her phone and shoved it into the pocket in her pants. Then she tried opening the doors again a little more frantically.

Her fingers were frozen and snow was quickly piling up on her as she pounded on the doors. Surely there was still someone in the office. She cupped her red, frozen hands and tried to look through the dark glass.

She kicked the doors and was just about to take out her cell phone to call 911 when the door was yanked open and she was pulled inside and engulfed in warm arms.

"What the hell do you think you're doing?" Aiden growled in her ear. "Trying to freeze to death?" He started to run his hands up and down her bare arms.

"N-n-no." She glanced at him, trying to pull away.

"You're frozen. How long were you out there?" He quickly removed his jacket, but instead of putting it over her shoulders, he laid it on the small credenza next to the balcony doors, and pulled her back into his chest and continued to rub her back and arms.

"N-n-not that l-l-long." She hated that her mouth wasn't cooperating. And that her teeth wouldn't stop chattering.

He looked down at her and then reached up and brushed the snow from her hair. When his fingers brushed over her hair for a fourth time, she closed her eyes and enjoyed the feeling of being touched.

Then she noticed just how hot his body temperature was. Maybe she'd been colder than she'd thought. She found it hard to believe that it had taken her this long to notice how muscular his body was.

His arms kept rubbing her, up and down. When they slowed a little, she let out a moan.

When she opened her eyes, she realized he was watching her. His dark eyes were glued to hers, and before she knew or expected it, his lips were on hers in a kiss that sent warmth to every part of her body.

Kristen had been kissed plenty of times in her life, but nothing could ever compare to the mouth that was covering hers now. His lips were soft, yet as they moved over hers, she felt the power behind them.

When he opened his mouth and used his tongue against her lips, she couldn't stop herself from enjoying the richness, the excitement, of his kiss. She opened for him, taking just a moment to relax against his warmth. His taste was something she could get used to, fall into, and get lost in.

He pulled back a little and frowned down at her. That's when she started shaking. Or maybe she had been shaking all along and had just realized it.

"I'm taking you to the hospital." He started to pull away.

"No." She grabbed hold of his arms. "Really, I was just out there for a moment. I just need to warm up." She smiled at the realization that her teeth were no longer chattering.

"Fine." He continued to rub his hands up and down her arms. "Do they have something hot to drink around here?" He glanced around, looking a little annoyed.

"Hot chocolate." She nodded toward the small break area that housed a large fridge, a microwave, and some cupboards full of dishes and supplies.

He leaned over and picked up his jacket, then placed it over her shoulders and wrapped his arm around her as they walked toward the break area.

It was dark in the back part of the building, so he flipped on the lights as they went.

"What are you doing here so late?" he asked as he rummaged through the cupboards, looking for what he wanted.

Her teeth started chattering again now that she'd lost his warmth. "I n-needed to finish up some changes for the Market Place job."

He glared at her over his shoulder. "Why were you out on the balcony in the snow, without a jacket?" He filled up a cup with water and shoved it into the microwave.

"I had a phone call." She closed her eyes and remembered the call.

"From?" He turned and pulled out a box of cocoa mix.

"A thief," she said and chuckled.

He dropped the mix and walked over to her and felt her forehead and then looked at her like she was crazy.

"It's a long story." She sighed and leaned back against the wall.

"I've got all night." He smiled.

She rolled her shoulders, trying to get her body to relax a little. "My ex-boyfriend."

He crossed his arms over his chest, showing her that he wasn't going anywhere.

She croaked, "I'd like something warm to drink first." She nodded toward the microwave, which had just beeped.

He busied himself with mixing the drink, then carried it over to the small conference room and set it down on the table. She sat down and took a tentative sip. It wasn't too hot, so she took another sip. The warm liquid felt like heaven.

"Go on." He sat next to her and she could tell that he wasn't going to leave her alone until he'd heard every detail.

CHAPTER
SIX

He listened as she told her story of how her ex-boyfriend had wiped her out. He was taken aback by how trusting and naive she'd been. To date, he'd never allowed someone to sleep over, let alone trusted another person with a key to his place.

"You're lucky he didn't murder you in your sleep."

She finished the mug of hot cocoa, and he noticed that her normal coloring had returned to her hands and face.

"I've learned my lesson." She frowned and looked down at the empty mug. He could tell she was hiding something.

"What?" He leaned forward and waited.

"What?" She glanced up at him through her eyelashes.

He arched his eyebrows. "There's something else."

"Actually, I've written off all men for a while. Especially after Christian." She waved her hand like she was shooing away a fly.

"Christian was the thief?" he asked.

She shook her head, so he waited. She sighed.

"Rod was the thief. Christian came after."

"What happened with him? Was he an abuser, a murderer?"

She groaned. "Oh no, he was a complete gentlemen." She rolled her eyes. "That was until I bumped into him and his wife and two kids."

He watched her face closely for hurt, but all he saw was frustration.

"Men are scum," she said, looking down at her hands.

He chuckled a little. "Sounds like you have a knack for catching the bottom dwellers." She glanced up and looked at him. "Not all men are thieves or adulterers," he assured her.

"I'm sure there are some decent ones out there, I've just sworn off trying to find them for a while." She stood up and picked up the mug. "Thanks. For everything." She turned to go.

He rushed over and took her shoulders in his hands. "What about dinner?" he blurted out.

Her dark eyebrows arched.

"I mean . . ." He was usually smoother than this. "Since it's late, why don't we grab some food, that way I can make sure you're fully recovered."

She sighed. "Thanks, but I've got—"

"It's just food. We can eat downstairs, if you want." When she looked like she was going to refuse him again, he added, "Listen, I don't usually admit this, but I hate eating alone. Since my last meeting ran long and it's too late for me to make something at home—I'm past starving at this point—I thought we could just grab something together. I'll buy."

She bit her bottom lip. "What about that kiss?" she said softly.

He shrugged. "It did the job of warming you up." He smiled and she smiled back.

Then she nodded. "Fine, but I have to finish printing the changes for our meeting first."

He agreed. "Fair enough. I need to grab some stuff too."

Less than half an hour later, they walked into the restaurant downstairs. Her clothes and hair had dried a little. Her hair hung down past her shoulders in a curly mass. He was happy to see that she'd pulled on a large coat over her dress shirt and slacks and had changed into heavy black boots.

"Do you walk to work every day?" he asked after they'd been seated near the windows that overlooked the Sixteenth Street Mall.

She shook her head quickly. "I ride the rail." She glanced at him over her menu. "You?"

"The bus drops me off in front of my condo. The train? You must live a little south of here?"

"Lincoln Park area."

He smiled. He had really liked the area and had thought about getting a place near there himself. "I looked at a condo there but chose one just a few blocks from here instead. When the weather is bad, I hop on the Sixteenth Street bus. But in the summer I can walk everywhere."

She set her menu down. "That's the nice thing about living downtown." She glanced up at him and he watched her cheeks turn a little pink. "Do you live alone?"

He tried to hide the smile. "Yes, you?" he asked.

She picked up her menu again and nodded.

"How long have you been in Denver?" he asked, enjoying the way she nibbled on her bottom lip when he asked her a question.

"Almost two years. After I finished school, I moved downtown." She rested back in her chair and set down her menu.

"Where from?" He leaned a little closer to her, wishing he could feel the softness of her skin again.

"Golden. You?"

"Originally, Littleton. I've been downtown for almost five years." Just then the waiter walked up and saved him from answering any more questions about himself.

After ordering, he asked her where she'd gone to school and how she'd gotten the job at R&S. He hung on to every word and had more questions he was dying to ask her.

He couldn't explain it, but he wanted to know everything about her. Maybe to help him figure out what was drawing him to her so much.

By the time their dinner arrived, he knew more about her than he'd known about his last five ex-girlfriends combined. He didn't understand why it still wasn't enough.

He tried to ask as many questions about her during their meal, without sounding desperate. She had answered every one and had even asked him a few herself. He did notice she had stuck to asking him about work, instead of personal topics.

By the time their meal was over, he still felt like he wanted to know more and didn't want to let her go just yet.

"The least I can do is walk you to the train station," he said as they stepped out into the night. The snow had yet to let up and he was thinking they'd have around a foot of fresh stuff by morning.

"Really, I'm all right now." She tucked her hair into her coat hood. When she shoved her hands into her pockets, he frowned down at her.

"You should have gloves," he said as he put his own winter gloves on.

She rolled her eyes. "Yeah, I have a nice new pair that Amy bought me just last week, but I couldn't find the left one." She shrugged. "I think I might have left it on the train."

"With your winning ticket?" he teased. He watched her lips turn downward and noticed the sad look in her eyes.

"Sorry," he mumbled.

"No, it's okay. I'm over it." She shook her head slowly, but he could still see the sadness in her eyes.

"You're not a very good liar." He chuckled.

Her smile fell away. "Lately, I'm not very good at a lot of things."

Reaching down, he pulled his gloves off and handed them to her.

"What?" She tucked her hands deeper into her pockets. "I can't take your gloves."

"Listen, I have a short bus ride, since I'm only a few blocks down. You have a wait at the train station, and then who knows how long of a walk it is to your place. Take them. Return them if you want. I have a few other pairs at home."

He nudged the gloves closer to her and she looked down at his hands. Then she sighed and reached out to take them.

"I'll return them tomorrow. I can stop by the store on the way to work and buy another pair. I guess I'll see you tomorrow." She turned to go.

"I wanted to meet with you a few minutes before we head out to the Market Place site," he said, feeling the need to say more, to keep her talking until the train came.

She nodded as she slipped his large gloves over her small hands. "I'll be at the office about an hour ahead of the meeting." She glanced up at him. "We can head out to the site together from there."

He turned and stopped walking. "Here comes your train now."

"Thanks." She looked back toward him. "For saving me from freezing, for dinner, for the gloves."

He smiled. "Anytime."

He watched her rush toward the train and hop on.

◆　◆　◆

It was funny how a day could start out completely terribly and end on a high note. She remembered the kiss and felt her face heat, then looked down at the soft leather gloves. Her fingers felt like heaven in the warmth of them. Even though they were too big for her, she couldn't get over how nice it had been of Aiden to lend them to her. And to buy her dinner, for that matter.

She'd enjoyed talking to him and had felt like she'd gotten to know a little more about him. At least she was starting to believe he wasn't a psychopath or, worse, married.

Still, she couldn't quite call what she felt for him attraction. At least, not the kind that she'd experienced before.

Sure, he was handsome. But she'd never really fallen for the tall, dark, and in charge kind before. No, what usually got her heart skipping was the blond beach bum.

She frowned as she looked down at the gloves. Maybe that had been her problem all along. What she wanted wasn't necessarily what she needed.

She thought about the dinner and about Aiden the entire trip home. By the time she walked into her apartment, with two new gloves, she had decided to keep an open mind about Aiden.

Of course, she needed her best friend's opinion on the matter. So she picked up her phone and dialed her.

"You did what?" Amy sounded like she was running through a tunnel.

"I decided to keep an open mind about Aiden."

"Who's Aiden?" She heard Amy ask.

"He's new at R&S."

"And? What does he do there?" Her friend's tone told her she was expecting another bomb to go off.

"Um, well, I don't actually know. No one does. Only that he's here on a temporary basis until he's not." She realized that he'd been too busy asking her questions during dinner to answer any of the ones she'd directed at him.

"O-kay." Amy drew out the word. "What does that mean exactly?"

She sighed, feeling like a fool. Nothing like your best friend to make you realize you'd jumped the gun. "It just means that I've never gone for a dark-haired, brown-eyed guy before. You know, clean cut, wears a suit."

"He wears a suit?" Amy sounded interested for the first time.

"Yeah." Kristen frowned, thinking that she'd just walked into another trap. After all, all she knew about him was that his name sounded familiar and he was not her type.

"What's his name?"

"Aiden." She rested back against the wall as she sat on her air mattress.

"Aiden what?" She could hear the question in her friend's voice.

"Aiden Scott." Just saying the name out loud made her heart skip for some reason.

"And?"

"And what?" She rubbed her forehead.

"Kristen, don't make me come over there. I have an early meeting."

She giggled. "He's tall, has dark hair with a little curl to it, chocolate eyes that are hard to read, and totally not my type."

Amy was silent for a while. "I like him."

"What?" She sat up and blinked a few times.

"Oh, come on. He breaks the mold. He's nothing like the last three guys you've dated."

"I don't count Tyler." She closed her eyes, remembering how the first real man of her dreams had run off with his best friend, Jake.

"Honey, Tyler got to second base, he counts."

"No. He only dated me to confirm that he was gay. That doesn't count."

"Okay, but you have to admit, the beach-bum guys just don't work for you."

She sighed. "Yeah, somewhere out there is my perfect man."

"Just be careful with this one, okay?" Amy begged.

"Right." She felt like a fool. She didn't know Aiden's intentions, but she had a feeling she was being played again. Her history made her cautious.

When she finally hung up with Amy, she decided a long, hot bath was in order. By the time she pulled herself out of the water, her entire body was aching and she knew she was paying for the short time she'd been locked out on the balcony.

She swallowed two aspirin and drank another mug of hot cocoa before bed.

When the alarm went off early the next day, she groaned and pulled her sore body off the air mattress. Today was going to be worse than yesterday because she couldn't stop shaking. Calling in sick was not even possible, not when she was the one calling the shots at the meeting.

At least the meeting was early. After she was done, she could head straight home and take the rest of the day off to recuperate.

It took a lot of energy to pull on her clothes. She didn't even really think about what she was wearing; she just picked the warmest clothes she had. When she stepped outside, she shivered and felt like crying. It was still snowing. How could it still be snowing?

The short hike to the station usually didn't bother her, but today every bone in her body ached and every step felt like it could be her last. She even stopped in the little store on the corner to purchase a new pair of gloves and a hot cup of tea to help soothe her sore throat. But, as she stepped out again, even her new gloves did little to warm her from the cold wind. She tucked her free hand deep into her jacket's pockets, but still felt like the chill was pushing through her and nothing would stop it. Even her eyelashes seemed frozen. When she walked into the office, Carla stopped her in the hallway just as the feeling was coming back to her face.

"Oh my goodness. Are you sick?" She rushed over to Kristen and took her arm. "Why on earth did you come in today?" She reached up and felt her forehead. "You're burning up."

"I have a meeting with Bob and Mark this morning. Then I'm heading home and going to bed right after."

Carla shook her head. "You could have let someone else handle that."

She leaned a little on the countertop, feeling like she'd just run a marathon. "No, it's my baby." She silently wished for the day to be over.

"Well, don't push yourself too hard." Carla glanced over Kristen's shoulder and smiled. "Morning, Mr. Scott."

Kristen tensed, remembering the kiss, how his lips had felt against hers. She felt her face heat and hoped that Carla didn't notice.

"Morning, Carla." She felt him stop just behind her. "How are you?"

"Oh, I'm just fine." Carla dragged out the words.

Kristen felt Aiden take her elbow and turn her a little. "What the . . . ?" His dark eyes changed and she could see concern in them. "I knew I should have taken you to the hospital yesterday," he said in a low voice.

"I'm fine, it's just a cold. It'll be gone by tomorrow," she said, trying to catch her breath, which she still couldn't seem to get under control. At least she was starting to feel less like a Popsicle.

"What on earth are you doing here?" he asked as he walked her toward the back break area.

"We have the meeting with—"

"Someone else can go," he interrupted her, then walked over and started pulling a mug out of the cabinet.

"I can handle my own meetings." She crossed her arms over her chest and frowned at his back as he heated up some hot water.

"Yeah, but in your condition you should be at home in bed rather than trekking through the snow and cold." He turned and looked at her and she watched him shake his head. "Fine, we'll go to the meeting, but you're going to bed directly afterward."

She felt like screaming that what she did was none of his business, but just then Paul walked in.

"Kristen, what have you done to yourself?" He rushed over to her and took her shoulders in his hands. "You look like death."

She wished she'd paid better attention to her reflection as she'd gotten ready that morning. Did she really look that bad? She glanced down and realized she'd pulled on some of her new clothes. They weren't inappropriate, but they were probably not the best choice for her meeting today. She had on a pair of dark blue dress slacks with a pale cream-colored blouse. The blouse probably highlighted her sickly coloring; she realized she must look horrid.

"I . . ."

"She's ill. I'll make sure she gets home directly after our meeting this morning."

Paul glanced over and nodded at Aiden. "Very well. Next time, give me a call. I'll send someone else out so you can rest."

She nodded and watched a hint of relief flood Paul's eyes before he turned and left. She was really starting to feel like a child.

"So, you'll take his advice, but you won't take mine?" Aiden said as he walked over and handed her the hot mug of cocoa.

"I've known Paul Stein all my life, and I just met you last week."

"Fair enough." He looked down at her lips as she took a sip.

"Besides, I know exactly what his motives are." She glanced at him over the mug and watched his lips curve into a smile.

CHAPTER SEVEN

Aiden kept stealing glances at Kristen during the meeting. He watched as her coloring went from pale to almost translucent. At one point, she looked green and when he reached over and took her arm to hold her steady, she glared at him.

By the time the meeting was winding down, she was no longer glaring at him as he held her upright. Her voice had grown softer and it looked like every breath she took caused her energy level to fall drastically.

"That's it; you're going straight to bed," he said, steering her toward the curb. The snow had finally stopped, leaving the streets full of slush. He was thankful she'd been wise enough to wear heavy snow boots and a warm coat. She'd even kept her new gloves on during the entire meeting.

"Yes, Dad," she said in a weak voice. When they jumped into the first taxi that stopped, she leaned her head back against the seat and closed her eyes as he told the cab driver his address. He didn't want her alone. Not until he made sure this time that she was okay.

He couldn't stop watching her. Her dark eyelashes contrasted sharply with her pale skin. He could see dark circles under her eyes and he frowned thinking about them.

He should have demanded that she go to the doctor yesterday after finding her trapped outside. He should take her to one now, but something told him that she'd use all her energy to fight it.

"I guess I fell asleep," she said, then let out a yawn as the cab stopped in front of his building.

"It's okay, we're here." He helped her out, then took her arm and smiled when she rested her head against his shoulder as they walked.

"I never get sick," she said as they made their way toward the warmth of the building.

"I only do when I don't get the flu shot." He nodded to the doorman and felt her stiffen next to him.

"Where are we?" She stopped and pulled her arms out of his.

"My place." He took her hand again. "You need rest and it's closer than us riding the train to your place."

She frowned. "I can get to—"

"Just humor me. I promised Paul I'd watch after you." He tugged on her hand, knowing she was too weak to fight it. "Besides, at this point, I doubt you could make it all the way home."

She sighed and closed her eyes, then swayed. He reached out to steady her.

"If you don't make up your mind quickly, I'll probably have to carry you upstairs. It's this, or I take you to the doctor's office a few doors down." Her eyes flew open and heated. Then she raised her chin and marched past him through the open doors. He smiled and followed her.

When he held his door open for her, her eyes grew large. "You live here?" She stood just inside his door, looking around.

"Yeah, you can explore later. Right now you need to get horizontal." He walked her back to his room. She closed her eyes as she sat on the edge of the bed. He tugged off her coat and tossed it over the chair near the window. Then he pushed lightly and she fell backward onto the bed. He pulled her boots off and set her legs on the bed.

She turned onto her side and he heard her moan.

"I only need to shut my eyes for a while," she said as she snuggled into his pillow. He took the throw blanket from the end of the bed and gently put it over her.

"Rest for as long as you need." He started to back out of the room.

She glanced up at him. "Just an hour."

He smiled. "Whatever you say." As he walked out, he flipped the lights off. He spent the rest of his day finishing up some of his own work.

When he made his way back into the bedroom again, five hours later, she was still sleeping. He touched her forehead and was pleased to see that her temperature had dropped back to normal.

She looked so small in his bed, so pale. Her hair was matted to her forehead and he reached over to brush it away from her face.

She really was unlike anyone he'd ever been attracted to before. Besides the looks, there was her intelligence. Kristen was smart and funny, and he was finding the mix intoxicating. He still couldn't understand the pull she had on him. Maybe it was the fact that she wasn't falling for him like most of the women he'd dated had.

In the last few months, he'd actually been on a dating hiatus of sorts. The couple of women he'd seen just before that had been so much . . . his type that he had been turned off. Maybe she was exactly what he needed. A change of pace.

He set a glass of water on the nightstand along with a bottle of aspirin and went to order delivery.

Half an hour later, he heard the water in his bathroom turn on and couldn't stop himself from imagining Kristen naked in his shower.

◆ ◆ ◆

Kristen stood under the hot spray and felt life seeping back into her bones. She'd never slept as hard or as comfortably as she had in Aiden's large, soft bed.

Just the thought of going home to her uncomfortable air mattress made her cringe.

When she stepped out of his spacious shower, she smelled something delicious coming from the next room. She frowned as her stomach growled for the first time that day. She'd been so preoccupied with making it through her meeting that she hadn't even eaten anything that morning.

She made sure to put everything back where she'd found it and then walked out of his bedroom fully dressed. She carried her boots since they were a little dirty and she didn't want to mess up his floors.

His place was impressive. She could only vaguely remember seeing the living room when they had come in. She remembered the view of the mountains. Now, as she made her way out of the bedroom, she noticed every detail. There was a sunken living area, a formal dining room, and a massive kitchen that sat near the back of the room. She couldn't really remember what building they'd gone into.

She didn't even remember what floor he was on, since she'd rested her head back in the elevator and tried not to pass out.

"It's good to see you up and alive." Aiden's voice came from the kitchen area. She walked into the room and found him sitting at the long bar. "I've ordered enough for two." He nodded to the Chinese delivery boxes that sat in front of him. "I hope you're hungry."

She thought about it and decided she could eat when she felt her stomach growl. "I am. Thank you." She walked over and set her boots by what she hoped was the front door. When she went back into the kitchen, she tossed her jacket over the chair.

"You've got your color back and your fever has broken. Feel any better?" He smiled as his eyes scanned her face.

"Yes. I'm feeling a lot better. Thanks again."

He began filling up her plate, and she was pleased to see that he'd ordered several of her favorite foods.

"I like your place," she said, sitting down along the bar area.

He moved over and sat next to her. "Thanks." She thought she saw something flash in his eyes, but she still couldn't read the mood in those dark eyes of his.

They sat in silence for a while as they ate. When she was full, she turned to him and watched him finish off his own plate.

"What are you doing at R&S?" she asked.

He thought about it for a moment, which only confirmed in her mind that he was hiding something.

"Helping a friend out," he said as he reached out to play with the tips of her hair. She leaned back, so his fingers came up empty.

"Why is working for them helping them?"

He shrugged and leaned closer to her. "There are different ways of helping out."

She narrowed her eyes as she looked at him. "You're a hard man to read," she blurted out and instantly wished she could take it back when he just smiled at her.

"I'll take that as a compliment." Her breath hitched as he reached out once more and touched her hair. His hand cupped the back of her head gently, and she felt shivers run down her spine and knew it had nothing to do with the flu she'd just battled. Then he tugged on her lightly, so she leaned closer to him. Her hands went to his thighs and she felt his muscles flex under her fingertips.

"I'm not interested," she said softly and felt her heart skip when he smiled slowly at her. Why hadn't she noticed how sexy he looked when he smiled before? Or how his mysterious eyes sparkled as he looked at her?

"The funny thing is, I don't know why I am either, but I figure, until I do, it couldn't hurt to explore." He leaned closer and she felt his breath mix with hers. His shoulders blocked out the light from the bar, almost giving him a halo around his dark hair. She could see slight highlights in the waves, making her want to push her fingers deep into it and explore the thickness and richness.

Her heart skipped a beat when his lips touched hers again. The kiss was nothing like the one he'd given her the day before. This time, there was a silent demand behind his soft lips.

She leaned closer to him and tried to match his pace. Her nails dug into his strong thighs as his fingers tightened in her hair. She moaned as she felt herself let go.

"This works for me," he said between kisses. When he tugged slightly, she slid off her stool and he drew her between his legs. She moaned as his hands ran down her sides.

Maybe it was because she'd told herself not to get this close to another man again, but she couldn't stop her heart from beating faster as her desire for him grew. A low moan escaped her when he pulled lightly on her hair and brushed his mouth over her neck.

"Yeah, I just don't feel the attraction," he said sarcastically as he licked his way back up to her lips.

She shivered and stroked her fingers lightly over his shoulders. She closed her eyes as her head rolled back, giving him access to her neck again.

"Tell me to stop," he said against her skin. "Tell me to go to hell." When he pulled back, she looked into his dark eyes.

"I . . ." she started to say but just shook her head.

He scooped her up and tugged her closer, and she wrapped her legs around his hips as he pulled her onto his lap. She could feel his hardness pressed against her core and moaned with want.

Desire was something she was all too familiar with, but desire this fast, this big, was a whole new game. Her hands went to his hair as he feasted on her mouth. His hands roamed over every inch of her back and the curve of her butt as she slowly moved above him, with him, as his hips jolted with every rocking motion.

Images of them wrapped together flooded her mind, and she dreamed about how good it would feel for her bare skin to be touched again.

When her cell phone buzzed in her coat next to her, she jumped and almost fell off his lap.

"Easy." His hands went to her hips to steady her.

She took a couple cleansing breaths. "Sorry." She reached over and took her phone out of her coat pocket.

Seeing Amy's number, she sighed. "I'd better take this." He nodded.

She pried herself off his lap, walked over toward his large windows, and punched Answer.

"Hey, I heard from my mom, who heard it from Michael, who heard it from his dad, that you were sick today. So I'm heading over to your place with some of my mom's homemade soup that she made for you."

"Um, that's really nice, but I'm feeling much better now." She bit her lip when she noticed how high up his place was. Just looking down made her knees turn a little weak.

"That's good to hear. Oh well, I'm also bringing over a movie so we can eat soup and hang out a little." She thought about the lack of furniture in her place and how uncomfortable her home was. She was still turned off every time Amy tried to drag her into a furniture store.

"Um, well, I'm not exactly at home right now."

"Okay, I'll pick you up. Where are you?"

She turned and looked at Aiden. "Um, downtown. How about you pick me up at work in . . ." She glanced down at her watch and almost did a double take. It was almost seven in the evening. "Half an hour?"

"Sounds good. I'll meet you out front where I normally get you. I hate finding a parking spot."

"Okay, see you then." Amy hung up and Kristen wished more than anything that she could read Aiden's expression. She was somewhat thankful for the interruption. After all, jumping into relationships hadn't worked out so great for her in the past.

"Hot date?" he said, leaning back on the counter.

"Worried friend. She's bringing homemade soup and a movie."

He smiled. "Sounds like a good friend."

"The best." She walked over and picked up her coat. "Well, thanks again . . ." She almost squealed when he pulled her back into his arms and kissed her quickly.

"There, now it's not so weird." He held her close. "And you know where we stand." She swallowed slowly. "Don't thank me." He frowned when she opened her mouth again. She shut her mouth quickly. "If you don't feel up to working tomorrow, make sure to call in sick instead of running yourself down."

"I don't have any meetings tomorrow."

"Good. How about dinner this weekend?"

She frowned. "Like a date?" His hands were on her hips, holding her close to him. For some reason, she was having a hard time thinking straight.

"I'd very much like to spend some more time with you."

She tilted her head and thought about it. "I guess so."

He shook his head and smiled at her. "Good, let's say Friday."

"Friday is happy hour. The first Friday of every month the employees go to Reds down the street for drinks after work."

"Then Saturday?" he asked.

She shrugged. "We can always go out after Reds."

"Then it's a date for Friday and Saturday." He kissed her one more time. "I'll take you back to the office."

He started to get up.

"You don't have to." She pulled on her coat.

"I know." He grabbed his coat, which hung above her boots. "But I will, just the same."

She walked over to put her boots on.

When they stepped outside, she was shocked to feel the warm air hit her.

"Colorado." He chuckled. "If you don't like the weather, wait five minutes."

"I know." She laughed. "Watch, it will be in the low seventies tomorrow."

"Fine with me. It would melt all this stuff away." He kicked at some of the snow with his boot and then reached over and took her hand. "We can walk, if you're up to it."

She looked around and was surprised to recognize that they weren't that far from the office. They walked in silence for a while, and she felt completely comfortable holding his hand walking down the crowded street.

"There's Amy." She waved toward Amy's car, which was parked in a tow-away zone near the back of the building.

"Well, I'd say that I hope to see you tomorrow, but I really don't since I think you should spend the day in bed." He pulled her closer and brushed the hair from her face.

"Thanks again." She could feel Amy's eyes on them from across the street and just knew she'd have a million questions to answer when she got in the car.

He dipped his head down and placed a kiss on her lips, which warmed her straight to her toes. "Just to make sure there's no lingering weirdness."

"The only weirdness is what I'll experience in the next few hours explaining that kiss to my friend."

She could feel his eyes on her as she dashed across the street and got into her friend's car.

CHAPTER
EIGHT

The next few days, Aiden tried to stay busy. Not only did he have research to do on R&S, but he had a few of his own projects that were quickly approaching deadlines.

He was pleased when Kristen hadn't shown up for work that following day, even though he desperately wished to see her again. When she did finally arrive at work two days later, she looked back to her normal self.

When he'd bumped into her in the hallway, she hadn't tried to avoid him or make it weird. Though he didn't like that she'd acted as if nothing had happened between them.

He, of course, tried not to remember how hard it had been to sleep in his bed after she'd been in it. When he'd gone to bed that evening, he could smell a subtle hint of her natural scent. He'd tossed and turned the entire night as he dreamed about holding her, kissing her, making love to her slowly.

He was really looking forward to the weekend so he could spend some time with her. He planned on having her over to his place again, which was totally out of the ordinary for him.

Actually, thinking about it, she was the first woman he'd had over to his place. The first one to actually sleep in his bed, for that matter. He laughed at the irony of it, since he hadn't even been lying next to her at the time.

When Friday finally came, the day seemed to slow to a stop as he waited for five o'clock to roll around, anticipating the upcoming evening. He noticed that everyone worked harder and faster as they tried to make the day go by quickly. Even he tried to keep himself occupied.

Finally, it was just a few minutes until he could clock out and join the rest of the crew at the popular bar down the street. As he was shutting down the workstation, he wondered how he could get Kristen alone for the rest of the evening.

"Are you going with us to Reds?" Carla walked into his office.

He glanced up at the blonde woman and his chin almost dropped when he noticed her outfit. Normally, she wore business-casual attire, but today her skirt was tighter and her shirt dipped dangerously low, showing off a very impressive chest.

He nodded in answer and then quickly turned back to his computer.

"Good." He heard her voice getting closer and tried not to think of how ironic it was that Carla was more his type than Kristen. But he'd never felt the pull toward her like he felt for Kristen. "It just wouldn't be the same if everyone weren't going," she said in a low voice. "Besides, I was looking forward to getting to know you better." She leaned on his desk right beside him. Her short skirt hiked up, and he tried to avoid glancing downward.

"I promised Kristen I'd go." He watched Carla pout.

Then she ran her well-manicured fingernail up his arm. "It's such a shame that she'll probably be stuck working late." She tensed.

"Late?" He leaned away, putting a little space between them.

"Oh yeah. The site on Market Street ran into some issues with the inspector. She's having to put in a bunch of hours this weekend to get everything ready for Monday."

He sighed. "I'd better go see if she needs any help." He started to get up but stopped when he noticed Carla hadn't moved aside. He'd have to climb over the top of her just to stand up.

"You're still going to Reds, aren't you?" He watched her bottom lip push out. She must have put on fresh lip gloss to make her lips shine so much.

"Not if there's work that needs to be done." He stood, pushing his chair all the way back to make enough room in the closed-in space.

"Oh well." She blinked a few times and he could tell she was desperately trying to think of another way to convince him to go.

Had he really been dating this kind of woman for the last few years? Why? He felt that his eyes were open for the first time, and there was no way he'd ever fall for tricks like the ones Carla was pulling. Maybe he'd just allowed himself to be played? Or maybe he'd just played along to get what he'd wanted?

"I'd better go." He nodded toward her legs, which were blocking his path.

Her smile grew as she stood up and ran a finger over his chin. "I'll save you a spot at the bar." She practically purred it.

When he finally made it out of his office, he took a deep breath of fresh air. Not only had the woman been taking his space, but she'd filled his whole office with the scent of her overbearing perfume.

When he walked into Kristen's cubicle, he could see she was deep into making changes. She didn't even know he was there, and he watched her work for a few moments. He glanced over her shoulder, and when he sat on the edge of her desk, she didn't even budge.

Finally, a few minutes later, she saved the design and leaned back. Her arms went over her head as she stretched her neck one way, then the other. Instantly, he felt the pull of attraction. Her soft scent was drifting his way and it took all his willpower not to move forward and bury his face in her hair.

"Well?" she said without turning around. "Thoughts?"

He scanned her work. "Nice." He wondered how long she'd known he was there.

She turned and looked at him. "Didn't you want to go with the rest of the gang to Reds?"

He glanced around and realized the place had emptied out. Shaking his head, he motioned to her screen. "Is that it or do you need to make changes to the back room as well?"

She frowned and looked back at her monitor. "Yeah, I was going to come in tomorrow and get that done."

"Working during the weekend sucks," he muttered, remembering all the long weekends he'd spent alone at the office. More importantly, how many relationships his long hours had broken up.

"Not always. I like being here alone. Fewer distractions. Plus, I can play my music as loud as I want and no one is here to complain."

"We can still make it to Reds if you want," he said, glancing at his watch. Not that he wanted to join the others, but he figured he needed to see if she wanted to go.

She bit her bottom lip, then said, "I'm sure Carla has saved you a spot."

"I wondered if the whole office had heard her invitation."

She rolled her eyes. "Don't get too flattered. She invites every new male employee."

"And here I was thinking I was special." He really wanted to spend more time with Kristen.

"I guess working here should come with a warning label."

He reached over and brushed a finger down her face slowly. "It does have its perks."

◆　◆　◆

What was she doing? More importantly, how had she allowed Aiden to talk her into forgoing happy hour and having a private dinner with him? A very romantic private dinner.

She'd never eaten at the restaurant before, nor had she known it existed. They were on one of the top floors of some very large hotel in what appeared to be a semiprivate dining room. There was a large swimming pool, covered for the winter season, just outside of the glass walls.

The dining room only held a half-dozen tables. There was a small bar area near the front doors and every seat was taken by well-dressed people.

"How did you find this place?" she asked, looking around after they were seated and their drinks had been delivered.

"A friend owns it." He smiled at her over his menu. "Actually, she's close friends with my mother."

"Oh?" She tried to hide her curiosity.

"Yes, they went to college together in Colorado Springs."

She wanted to ask more questions about his family but couldn't bring herself to do so yet. Who was she kidding? She couldn't hold back the questions.

"What does your mother do?" she finally asked as she set down her menu.

"She's in real estate. What about your parents?"

"Mom works in loan approvals at the Veterans Affairs. My dad is a family physician in Golden." She glanced at him. "What about your father?"

"My real father is somewhat of a recluse." He shook his head.

"Oh?" She leaned back after taking a sip of the wine he'd ordered for them. For some reason, she felt like melting.

"He divorced my mother when I was four, moved into the mountains, and married a woman half his age."

"That must have been hard on you."

His eyebrows rose. "Not really. My mother took it hard for a while, but then she met my stepfather, Eric, and they've been happy ever since. Eric and I get along great. Actually, better than I do with my real father."

"Do you visit him often? Your real father, I mean."

"No, last time I was up there, Dad almost shot me for trespassing. I think he's fallen a little off his rocker."

"I'm sorry. My great-uncle raised snakes." He looked at her. "He had over a thousand of them in his house. He separated them out—poisonous and nonpoisonous. They filled his entire house." She cringed remembering the smell. "Next to his bed was a huge cage that held a ten-foot boa constrictor named Dolly."

"Okay, so I'm not the only one with crazy in my blood."

"Amy's aunt thinks she's the long-lost daughter of Hemingway."

"Really?" He leaned his elbows on the table.

"I've met her." She made a circle motion next to her forehead. "She's really off her rocker."

He chuckled just as the waiter walked up. After ordering, they continued to compare notes on crazy family members. She enjoyed finding out a little more about him. He had two younger half sisters named Amber and Ashley. Since he was so much older than them, he had basically been their babysitter until he'd finally moved out and gone to school. He sometimes called his stepfather his father, which reinforced that he did really like the man.

"Your family sounds wonderful." She pushed her almost-empty plate away. The wine and the food were causing her to relax.

"Yeah, I guess I lucked out in that area." He poured her more wine.

"You are very difficult to figure out," she said after taking another sip of her wine. She knew it would most likely be her last since she was starting to feel tipsy and light-headed. "I mean . . ." She shook her head.

He chuckled. "Not really. I'm pretty cut and dry."

"No, you're not. I mean, most men, I think that I have a good handle on them—"

He laughed before interrupting her. "After hearing your track record, I'd say you're usually pretty far off."

She groaned, "I guess that's true, but still . . ." She leaned back again and crossed her arms over her chest. "I don't usually find myself attracted to someone like you. I guess maybe I was due for a change, but I have such a hard time reading you that I'm unsure."

He frowned, then reached over and took her hand in his. "Let's get out of here."

She sighed and just looked at him.

"No, I mean, this is a conversation for someplace a little more private. Don't you think?"

She glanced around and realized the place was packed. There were people standing at the bar and she could see a line out the door for people waiting to sit down for dinner.

Nodding, she grabbed up her stuff and followed him out to the elevators. "Where to?" she asked when they walked out onto the street. He took her hand in his and started walking down the outside mall.

"I know this may be a little forward, but how about my place?" He glanced at her sideways.

She stopped walking, and when he turned toward her, she looked at his eyes. She could tell he had been sincere, but something in his face told her he was feeling the same thing she was. Desire.

"That is pretty forward." She couldn't stop herself from teasing him.

His smile was quick. "We can just talk. Honest." He held up his hand, palm toward her.

"No Scout's oath?" she teased further.

He shook his head. "I was too busy watching my sisters to join the Scouts."

"What did you say your parents did all the time that left you alone with your sisters?"

"They each headed up a few major charity events for the country club, not to mention they were always traveling for work."

She thought about it, about him, about being with him, and something inside her kicked. "All right, but I can't stay long. I do have to put in a couple hours tomorrow."

He took her hand and started walking again. "You know, if you need any help tomorrow . . ."

"No, most of the changes the inspector required were in the front. The HVAC system in those old buildings can be a real pain to work around."

"I worked on this project once where it took us four different inspections to finally get everything right. We had to tear out three walls."

"But saving historic buildings can totally be worth it," she added.

He nodded as they walked toward the doors to his building.

She stopped and looked up. "I didn't get to appreciate this the last time I was here. They don't make them like this anymore."

"For a good reason. The cost alone would drive the rent sky-high."

"I suppose. What floor are you on again?" she asked as they walked in.

"Twenty-fifth. I got a great deal on the place." He held open the elevator door for her. "Now everyone wants to live in the newer loft buildings that are popping up all over."

"Isn't this one of the oldest high-rises in Denver?" she asked.

"Yes, it was abandoned for over thirty years until an investor snatched it up and started remodeling and selling one floor at a time.

"Whoever it was did a great job," she said, trying to hide her nerves about the thoughts that were rushing through her mind. She knew she wanted more than just conversation. Much more.

"I'm just lucky this place became available when it did," he said, stepping out of the elevator after her.

He pulled out his keys to open his door. Then he stood back as she walked in.

CHAPTER NINE

Kristen strolled into his place, and he could see her nerves from across the room. Somehow seeing her fidget made him feel a little more confident.

"Do you want something to drink?" he asked.

She turned and glanced at him. "Something hot would be nice."

"Coffee?" he asked as he moved toward the kitchen.

"Sounds good," she said and then turned back to his view. "I bet this is great during the day."

"I can see all the way down to Pikes Peak on a clear day." He flipped on the coffeemaker and went over to get two mugs.

She made her way back and leaned on the bar, watching him. "Why do you rattle me?" She sat down on a stool.

"From what you tell me of your past, you have a reason to be rattled."

She shook her head. "No, it's funny. With the other men, I was more sure about pursuing a relationship."

He arched his eyebrows. "Is that what we're doing?"

She shrugged. "I'm not the kind that sleeps around."

"Agreed. Neither am I." He watched her eyebrows shoot up in question and couldn't help chuckling. "That's probably hard to believe, but it's true. I've had my share of exes, but all of them were fairly long relationships."

"What's long?" She rested her elbows on the countertop.

He leaned back on the counter, crossed his arms over his chest, and thought about it. "Cindy was the shortest and that relationship lasted almost seven months."

Her chin dropped, and then she quickly recovered.

"What about you?"

"Rod was my longest at three months." She felt her face flush a little.

"Rod, the one that stole all of your stuff?" he asked.

She looked down at her hands.

"Okay. So it sounds like I've got you beat." He smiled. "Maybe I should be the one questioning your intentions."

She laughed. "Okay, you may have me there. I've had rotten luck with relationships." She frowned a little and he turned around to pour them each a cup of coffee.

"Black?" he asked over his shoulder. She nodded.

"Actually, my luck in other areas hasn't been all that great for a while either." She followed him into the living area and settled into his soft leather sofa with her coffee.

"You may think I'm crazy, but the worst of it started a little over a year ago, right after I started working at R&S full time." She took a sip and held her mug in both hands. "I had started seeing this guy that I'd gone to school with. We'd only gone out a few times as friends, but I was hoping that it would turn into something more." She took another sip of the coffee. "I didn't know that his sister was a Wiccan."

"For real?" He leaned closer just a bit, wanting to hear more.

"Well, it turned out that our first official date fell on her birthday. And when her brother decided to spend the evening with me, she hunted us down at a local club and, in front of a dozen or more people, cursed me."

He tried not to laugh. Really, he did. "Do you believe in that stuff?"

She shrugged, but her eyes turned sad. "Not really. I mean, no. But

I just can't explain how after that night, my luck has taken a turn for the worse."

He reached over and brushed a strand of her honey-colored hair away from her face. "We make our own luck. Good or bad."

"I'd like to believe that, but I would also like to believe that I'm not that big of a klutz."

"My sister Ashley went through a phase in middle school. She broke her arm at the beginning of the year, then her foot six months later. It seemed that every time we turned around, she was getting into trouble."

"And?" She moved next to him and he enjoyed the smell of her perfume.

"She grew out of it."

She sighed as she shook her head. "I'm not some teenager who's just going through a phase."

"Trust me, I know you're not." He enjoyed watching her eyes heat when he touched her.

"I'm having a really hard time avoiding this. Avoiding you," she whispered.

"Then don't," he said as he leaned forward and kissed her. He knew the kiss affected her as much as it did him when he felt the moan vibrating from her. He couldn't stop his hands from pulling her closer. He wanted to feel her body pressed up against his. Her hands went to his hair, holding him close to her as he used his mouth to show her what he wanted.

"This is crazy, how much it affects me," she said against his neck.

"Let it," he mumbled. Then he ran his hands over her body as she arched to give him better access. She was so soft and he wanted to touch her everywhere. "Enjoy. I know I am."

He loved the feel of her fingers exploring him, tugging off his jacket. He leaned back and tossed it over the sofa, then went to work on her shirt. It was a long blouse with ridiculously small buttons down the front.

She giggled and then helped him. "Amy's choice."

He lost his breath when she pulled it off and sat in front of him in nothing but a silky bra and her slacks.

"Beautiful," he whispered as he reached out with a shaky hand to touch her gently.

Her eyes closed and her head fell back as she moaned.

"So soft." He moved closer to her and dipped his head to taste her skin.

When he looked up again, her eyes locked with his as she reached over to tug off his button-up shirt. He watched her eyes heat when she pulled it off and tossed it next to his jacket.

He moaned lightly as she ran her fingers over his chest slowly.

"Impressive." Her fingers touched every inch, and then she shocked him by running her mouth where her fingers had just been. His hands went to her hair as a moan escaped his lips.

"You're driving me nuts here. I'm trying to be good." He leaned back and felt a shiver run through his body.

"You had no intention of being good." She leaned up and kissed him. "Neither did I."

♦ ♦ ♦

Kristen couldn't have stopped herself from wanting Aiden if she'd tried. Not after seeing what was underneath that suit of his. How had the man gotten a body like that? Even just running her fingers over him caused her pulse to double and her fingers to shake. She wanted to see what was under the rest of his suit.

She'd struggled with coming back to his place, knowing that if he kissed her, she would lose control. But after the wonderful dinner and spending time talking to him, her doubts had left her. He was unlike any man she'd known. There was a sense of integrity in him that she'd never experienced before, and it was making her crazy for him.

The way he was running his hands and mouth over her caused her entire body to shake with want. When he tugged lightly and moved her underneath him, she wrapped herself around him as much as she could, needing to be closer.

"I told you I wasn't going to do this," he said against her skin.

"We both knew you were lying." She smiled when he took her mouth again. The kiss heated her up from her core, spreading out to every inch of her body.

She felt his hard body above hers and locked her legs around his hips as he savored every inch of her exposed skin.

"Tell me to stop," he said as his fingers brushed just above the elastic in her slacks.

She closed her eyes on a slight moan and knew that if she asked, he would stop. But, did she want him to?

Shaking her head, she arched for him, showing him what she wanted. His fingers dipped lower as he unclasped the hook at her waistband and slowly ran the zipper down.

She moved up to help him slide the slacks off her legs. When his fingers moved down her legs, she heard him sigh.

"This is the first thing I noticed about you."

She glanced at him in question and watched him smile.

"Your legs." He was touching her bare skin like it was glass and would break. His touch sent goose bumps spreading everywhere. "Sexy as sin. They seem to go on forever." His hands ran higher until they reached her new silky panties.

When he brushed a finger over the softness, her hips jumped and she lost all thoughts except being with him.

"I want to take you into my room," he said, leaning back a little. His eyes were roaming over every inch of her.

"Hurry," she begged. She started to get up, but he surprised her by picking her up. She giggled nervously.

"You did say hurry." He grinned down at her as he walked.

She ran her fingers over his neck until he set her down gently on his bed.

"I couldn't sleep in here the other night, thinking about you lying here," he said against her skin. "Just the smell of your sweet perfume drives me nuts."

She slid her hands down and pulled off his slacks as she tugged him closer. He helped her undress him until he hovered above her, gloriously naked.

She realized then that she still wore her new panties and bra set. But when she reached to take them off, he shook his head.

"No, let me." Instead of pulling them off, he teased her by rubbing his hands over the silk until she closed her eyes and moaned with delight.

He was destroying her with his slow touches and passionate kisses, and she knew he was enjoying himself completely.

"You're so soft here." His fingertip touched her shoulder blade. "And here." He brushed over her sensitive skin just under the edge of the silky bra.

Her fingers dug into his shoulders as he used his hands and mouth to explore her slowly.

"Aiden." She could feel herself building too fast and wanted him—no, needed him—now. "Soon, darling." His mouth rubbed over her ribs and she felt him tug her panties off her legs. She tried not to gasp when his mouth found her heat. The feeling of him kissing her forced her shoulders off the bed as she gripped his hair and held on.

She retreated into her own private bliss as she felt every touch, every kiss, that he used to pleasure her. When she felt her body tense and saw the bright lights flash behind her eyelids, she couldn't stop the shaking that came next, nor did she try.

"Beautiful," he said, just over her. She kept her eyes closed and heard him tear open a condom package. "I want more." Then she felt his hands on her hips as he settled between her thighs. "Kristen, look at me."

She opened her eyes and smiled up at him. Her hands went into his hair as she pulled him closer. When he flexed his hips slowly, she couldn't stop the moan or the sigh from escaping her lips as he entered her in one smooth motion.

"More," she said as her nails dug into his hips when he just held still, deep inside her. "Faster," she growled out and nibbled on his ear when he started to move. She wanted the speed.

He moaned when her tongue darted out and licked him behind the ear. She felt his pulse jump, and then he was moving faster.

She'd thought she could easily stay in control—that was until she felt him pounding into her. His hips slapping against hers, his mouth covering her lips, taking every moan, every sound, as he pleased her. Opening her eyes, she looked up directly into his darker ones. Something kicked inside her as he watched her cry out his name.

She lost her breath and held on to him as he took what he needed and gave her pleasure beyond anything she'd ever experienced.

When she felt him stiffen above her, she held on to him and let herself join him.

She lay there and listened to his heartbeat settle and then slow down. He was crushing her, but it felt too good to ask him to move. It had been too long since she'd felt the weight of a man over her. Too long since she'd had multiple orgasms.

"I can hear you thinking from up here," he said against her skin. Then he leaned up on his elbows and looked down at her.

His hair was a mess from her hands and he had a sexy smile on his lips. His dark eyes looked a little dreamy and she was shocked to feel him growing inside of her again.

"I'm just running through my mind how wonderful I feel."

"I'll second that." He smiled at her as his hands ran up her sides. "You do feel wonderful." He leaned down and placed his mouth on her neck, nibbling up and down her skin.

She sighed and wrapped her legs around him again. "Mmm, more." She giggled and then moaned as his hips started moving again.

CHAPTER
TEN

"You can stay, you know." Aiden frowned at Kristen as he watched her pull on her shirt.

She glanced over at him. "Can't. I've got an early morning if I want to get those changes done in time."

He leaned down and picked up his pants, then tossed them over his chair and reached for a pair of worn jeans instead. When he turned around, she was watching him closely. He could see the heat in her eyes and wanted nothing more than to spend the entire night making love to her. "Are you sure?" He pulled on a white T-shirt and smiled when he watched her chin drop just an inch.

She nodded her head without blinking. "Yeah."

"It's a shame." He slowly started walking toward her and saw the heat turn her eyes a darker green.

He stopped right in front of her and placed his hands on her hips. She was small and he loved the softness of her.

"I can set the alarm?" He leaned down and placed a kiss on her lips, waiting to pull away after he felt her breath hitch. When he did pull back, he noticed that her eyes were closed and she was swaying just a little.

"I really shouldn't." She sighed and leaned her head against his chest. Then he watched her eyes open and she shook her head clear. "No, I'd better go." She blinked a few times and he could see she'd made up her mind.

"Fine, but meet me tomorrow for lunch." He held her still, pressed up against him. Her hands were on his chest and she was looking down at her fingers.

"Okay." She glanced up at him. "Text me where and when."

After she left, he was too wired to sleep, so he showered and got dressed. He figured he might as well kill a few hours and catch up with some of his own work.

Something kept nagging at him in the back of his mind. He wanted more than anything to tell Kristen what he was doing at R&S. But he knew it wasn't only the wrong time, but he'd made an agreement to keep it quiet.

It took him less than five minutes to walk to his design firm office building and key in. The place was dark except for a couple rooms. Some of his employees worked on their own schedule, so he stopped in and chatted with the few who were still working before he headed to his own office.

He stayed and tried to work until just past midnight, then headed home feeling defeated. The entire time he had tried to work, his mind had been occupied with Kristen.

He didn't know what had caused him to ask her to stay, but he desperately wished that she had. He wasn't looking forward to going home to an empty bed that was doused in her soft scent.

♦ ♦ ♦

The next morning, after a rough night of sleep, his mother called and wanted to meet him for breakfast since she was downtown.

When he walked into the restaurant and saw her and Eric sitting at a table near the front, he knew instantly something was wrong.

"Hi." He sat down and looked between them. "What's up?"

His mother looked at Eric, and he sighed. "It's about your father, Gordon."

He waited. The man hadn't really been a father to him. Not like Eric had been.

"Honey, he had a stroke last night," his mother cut in, holding back a sniffle.

"Is he . . . ?" he started to ask.

Eric shook his head. "No, he's at the hospital in Vail. We were going to go—"

"No, don't bother. I'll go up and see him," he interrupted. He couldn't quite get a handle on what he was feeling. There were too many emotions rushing through him at the same time. One thing was clear: he didn't think he could handle seeing his father alone. Only one person's face came into his mind.

His mother sighed. "I know it's been hard, not seeing him, but he's still your father." She glanced at Eric, who nodded in agreement. After everything that man had done to his mother, she still cried over him.

After two cups of coffee and a small bagel with blueberry cream cheese, Aiden kissed his mother on the cheek, shook Eric's hand, and headed out. There was one place he had to stop off first.

When he walked into the R&S offices less than an hour later, he could hear Kristen's music blasting through the entire floor. He smiled as he listened to Joan Jett's "I Love Rock 'n' Roll" all the way to Kristen's desk.

He stood behind her and watched her work until the song ended.

"That's looking good." He watched her jump as her head spun around with a shocked look on her face and instantly felt guilty.

"Sorry." He took her shoulders in his hands and started to rub the tension from them, then leaned on her desk. "Didn't mean to scare you."

She closed her eyes as she took a few deep breaths. "You didn't scare me. I always jump and have a panic attack when people come up behind me."

He chuckled and she glared up at him. Just watching her work had taken his mind off his personal issues. He knew he wanted to spend more time with her.

"Are you about done?" he asked as he ran a hand down her arm.

"Yeah, I'm just finishing up." She smiled for the first time and he felt his heart jump and his breath hitch like hers had a few moments ago when he'd startled her. "Want to do lunch?"

"I can't. Something's come up." He watched her green eyes turn dark. "I've got an errand to run and was kind of hoping you'd tag along."

She leaned back and crossed her arms over her chest. "What kind of errand?"

"My father had a stroke last night." Just the words on his lips caused his heart to sink and feel heavy.

"Oh." She leaned up and took his hands. "I'm so sorry."

"He's at the hospital in Vail, and I was hoping you'd go with me to visit him." He needed her there; for some reason he doubted he would be able to deal with his father if she wasn't by his side.

"Me?" She blinked a few times.

"Well, it's close to a two-hour drive up there. I figured you could keep me company." He knew it was starting to sound like he was begging, but he didn't care. Not if it got her to agree to go.

He could tell she was thinking about it, but she still had a slight frown on her lips.

"I've arranged for a hotel room so we won't have to drive back in the dark."

She looked at him and tilted her head, and he wished he knew what she was thinking.

"Honest, I'm not an ax murderer. You can call my mother and step-father to confirm." He held out his cell phone for her.

She looked at it and sighed. "I know you're not a murderer. It's just . . ."

"I know." He took her hands in his. "If you want your own room, I'll understand."

"It's not that." She bit her bottom lip, then asked, "How is your driving?"

He almost laughed. "I'm a very safe driver. No speeding tickets, no accidents. Well, none that I've caused. A mother of four backed her minivan into me in the shopping mall's parking lot once when I was twenty."

"I'll need to stop by my place first. Plus, I need to finish this up." She glanced back at her computer screen.

"We can get some lunch on the road after we swing by your place," he suggested.

"Sounds like a plan. Give me fifteen minutes to finish up here."

"I'll be in my office." He leaned down and kissed her solidly on the lips. "Thanks."

◆　◆　◆

"Tell me I'm not crazy," she whispered into her phone.

"No, not crazy. A little spontaneous, but not crazy," Amy whispered back.

"Why are you whispering?" She giggled and then glanced toward Aiden's office. "You're at home." Amy laughed. "I don't know. After what you told me happened last night—and let me tell you again how jealous I am about it—I can see why you'd be hyped to go. Just keep your phone on you and charged and text me every once in a while."

"Yes, Mother. I've got to go. I have to finish my work. He's waiting."

"Kris?" Amy broke in before she could hang up. She knew her friend only used her nickname when she wanted her attention.

"Yeah?"

"I know the trip is about his father, but try and have a good time too."

"I will." She finished up her work, smiling the entire time.

When they walked out of the building less than half an hour later, she felt nervous until he reached over and took her hand in his. They rode the bus back to his place and she sat on the edge of his bed as he packed a small bag for himself.

She groaned, remembering that she no longer had an overnight bag of her own.

"What's wrong?" He glanced at her.

"Um, maybe we can stop off at the store so I can get a bag." She tucked her hands into her pockets. "I haven't had time to replace a lot of my stuff that was stolen."

"He took everything?" he asked, and she could see concern in his eyes.

"Everything, except a few things hanging in my closet and some items in my kitchen."

He sat next to her. "I have another bag." He reached under his bed and pulled out a bag identical to his. "Here, you're welcome to it."

She smiled. "Thanks. Are you all packed?"

He nodded and then leaned closer and kissed her until she felt out of breath and her skin was heated.

"We'd better get going if we want to make it up there before dark." He helped her up off the bed.

She was a little surprised to see the shiny black BMW he stowed his bag in. When he opened the passenger door for her, she had to blink a few times to make sure she wasn't hallucinating.

What was an architect of his age doing driving a car like this? The leather seats were warm and felt like heaven as she watched him walk around the front.

"I like your car," she said when he started the engine up.

"Thanks, I just got it last year." He clicked on his seat belt and waited until she did the same. "Do you have a car?" he asked as he backed out of his spot in the parking garage.

"I had one a couple months ago." She remembered the disaster.

"Accident?" he asked.

"No, I got carjacked and they drove my new Mustang into a river."

He frowned and glanced at her as he pulled out of the building. "How terrible. You weren't hurt, were you?"

"Just my pride." She looked out the window as they headed toward her apartment.

Fifteen minutes later, they walked through her front door. She was so busy thinking about what she'd need to take that she hadn't thought about what her place looked like.

"You live here?" He took her hand and stopped her from walking back to her room.

"Um, yeah." She chuckled. "Okay, so I haven't had time to replace much of anything." She groaned. "Do you know how hard it is to find the right furniture?" She crossed her arms over her chest and sulked as she looked down at the two beanbags.

"At least tell me you have a bed," he said as he started walking toward her room.

"Of sorts," she said, catching up with him.

He stopped short just inside her room. "That?" He glanced at her. "You're sleeping on that?"

She frowned at the air mattress. "It's not as bad as it looks."

He turned to her. "Tell me the bastard is at least locked up."

She shook her head. His dark eyes had turned a deeper color and she could tell he was pissed. But he took her shoulders and tugged until she was in his arms.

"I'm sorry. I'm sorry the jerk did this to you," he said into her hair as she held on to him.

"It's not as bad—" she started, but stopped when she felt his head shaking no.

"First thing this week, I'm taking you to get furniture." He pulled back. "I know you're a designer, but I have a few connections that might help." He smiled down at her. "Besides, I love shopping for stuff."

"Right. And I suppose you love to cook and do laundry too."

"Cook, yes. Laundry, no." He tugged her farther into the room. "Now, pack." He handed her the bag and she got to work as he leaned against her wall and watched. She was a little self-conscious when she had to push aside her cotton panties to get to the fancy ones she wanted to take for him, but when she glanced at him, he was busy looking down at his phone.

When they finally drove out of Denver after eating a quick drive-through meal, she couldn't contain her excitement for heading into the Rockies.

"It's been almost a year since I've gone into the mountains." She watched the scenery whiz by. She'd really missed being engulfed in the hills. Surrounded by trees and rocks. The beauty of it all almost made her eyes water.

"A year?" He glanced at her. "You didn't go skiing this year?"

"With my luck?" She laughed.

CHAPTER
ELEVEN

Aiden loved driving, but he especially loved driving in the mountains. The freedom of flying up the road as the trees zipped by gave him pure pleasure.

Kristen sat next to him, quietly watching the scenery. When he thought about her empty apartment, he felt like hunting down that ex of hers. He couldn't imagine anyone living with as little as she had. But what really got him was imagining her sleeping on the small air mattress every night.

"How often do you ski?" she asked.

"I snowboard." He looked over at her. "Not as often as I want to. This winter I went around a dozen or so times."

"Where do you go?"

"Breckenridge. I have some land near there and a cabin that I share with my family."

"I like Breckenridge. I spent a week up there a couple summers ago with Amy. I've never been to Vail before, though."

"You'll like it. You should really go in early fall when all the aspen leaves are turning." Some of his best memories were in the Colorado Rockies.

"I've seen pictures, and I've seen the trees in other mountain towns."

"It's not the same as spending a warm autumn night sitting out on a blanket somewhere watching the leaves fall." He glanced out the window and could just imagine how it would look this fall. "We'll come up this fall and spend some time."

She looked over at him and he could see a little apprehension in her eyes, so he asked, "Does it scare you thinking about still being with me this fall?" He smiled when she blushed. "I know you're the kind that loves 'em and leaves 'em," he joked.

She laughed. "It's just strange listening to a man talk about commitment to a relationship. I haven't had that before."

He reached over and took her hand. "I think I've gotten a real sense for what you've experienced in relationships before. Especially after seeing your apartment."

"Yeah, well." She sighed and glanced out the window again. "So I haven't had any luck finding the right man. There are a lot of people out there like me. Amy has only been in one long-term relationship."

"I'm going to have to meet Amy one day soon." He wondered if she was anything like Kristen, or the complete opposite.

"She's telling me the same thing about you." She squeezed his hand. "You know, Amy wasn't all that impressed with my exes."

"I bet." That answered some of his questions about her best friend.

"What about your exes?" she asked.

He shrugged. "Well, you could sum up my relationships with only a few words." He brought her hand up to his lips and kissed her knuckles. "Dull, boring, repetitive." He kissed her hand again. "Maybe that's why I've found myself interested in someone who is completely different from what I'm used to."

The rest of the drive was peaceful. The clouds blocked out the sun outside of Vail, and by the time they drove up to the hospital, light rain was falling.

When they walked into the hospital, he felt nerves pounding through him. The last time he'd seen his father, the man had pointed a shotgun at him. Of course, he couldn't blame the man for not recognizing him. He hadn't seen him since he'd been a young teen.

"Are you all right?" Kristen asked, taking his hand in hers.

He looked down at their joined fingers and nodded. "Yeah. Just getting prepared."

"Do you know what room he's in?"

"Three twenty."

"There are the elevators." She motioned to the left. "Would you like me to go with you?"

He squeezed her hand. He couldn't imagine walking in to see his father without her. "If that's okay."

They walked over together, and she punched the button herself.

He stopped just outside of his father's room, dropped her hand, and took a couple deep breaths. Kristen stood beside him and waited.

When he reached for the door handle, it flew open quickly and a small blonde woman rushed out.

"Oh!" she said, taking a step back as she wiped her eyes dry.

"Hello, Shannon," he said to his father's second wife, who had been his babysitter for most of his childhood.

"Aiden." She gasped and glanced back with a frown. Then she stepped forward and shut the door behind her. "Does your father know you're here?"

"Not yet." His eyebrows shot up in question.

"Well, he's resting right now." She frowned again and looked down at her hands. "I . . . I don't think it's a good time."

"You've kept us apart for too long." He took her shoulders and gently nudged her aside.

"It's just . . ." She tried to stop him by putting her hand around his bicep. "He's in a mood."

Memories of his father flooded his mind. "Dad was always in a mood." He opened the door, took Kristen's hand again, and walked into the room.

"Damn it! I said get out!" He watched his father's face pale when he saw him. "Who the hell are you?"

"Is that any way to greet your long-lost son?" He walked over and stopped next to his father's bed.

◆　◆　◆

Kristen looked down at the older man in the bed and almost did a double take. Aiden had never mentioned that his real father was Gordon Harvey, the former Colorado senator. The man was a legend to most people who had lived in Colorado. The man had not only helped clean up Denver and clear out a lot of the gangs but had been singly responsible for keeping most of the big ski resorts open.

She stood next to Aiden and could feel his tension through his hand in hers.

"Aiden?" His father blinked a few times, and then irritation crossed the man's face. He looked thin and frail, and she guessed that he was paler than normal.

"Dad, how are you doing?" Aiden held her hand tighter.

The older man looked up at him. "I'll live. If they ever stop poking me." He waved his hand a little, exposing the tubes sticking out of them. "Damn doctors."

"This is Kristen Collins." He brought her a step closer to his father. "My father, Gordon Harvey."

"Mr. Harvey." She felt her heart kick a little.

"I didn't expect to see you here." He shifted in the bed, looking at his son.

"I had breakfast with Mom and Eric. They told me what happened."

"Shannon called them." The old man rolled his eyes, looking somewhat aggravated.

"Shannon?" Aiden asked, sounding a little confused.

"Woman never listens to me. I told her not to bother you." His father settled a little more on the bed.

"Shannon has been the one keeping me away from you. Why would she call?" Aiden asked.

"Shannon has been sheltering you," he answered and closed his eyes. "I haven't been myself lately. Actually, the last few years. They tell me it's Alzheimer's. Damn if I can remember most days. The drugs they have me on here make me even crazier."

Aiden shook his head, looking like he was unsure exactly what he was hearing. "Then, the last time I was in Vail?"

"Shannon told me I pointed the Remington at you." He opened his eyes and glanced at Aiden. "Sorry."

Aiden looked rooted to the floor. He turned to Kristen. "If you want, you can wait outside for a while."

She looked up at him, then nodded. Dropping his hand, she turned and walked out of the room. She knew Aiden needed some time alone with his father, especially since it appeared he was lucid. She could only imagine the pain of having to deal with someone slowly losing their mind.

When she stepped out, she noticed the small blonde woman from before was sitting across the hall. She could see the woman's eyes were red and that she'd been crying.

"Did he kick you out too?" she asked in between breaths.

"No, Aiden wanted some time alone with his father."

The woman patted the spot next to her. "You can sit if you want."

She smiled and walked over to sit next to her.

"I'm Kristen Collins."

"Shannon Harvey." She shook her hand. "I married Gordon shortly after Aiden's parents divorced."

Kristen wished she knew more about what had happened to Aiden's family but doubted it was nice to ask any questions.

"You two look real good together," Shannon said, wiping her nose on her tissue. "How long have you been together?"

"Well, we've actually worked together for a while."

"Oh." Shannon looked down at her hands.

"But recently started seeing each other," she added.

"That's nice," she said absentmindedly as she watched the nurses walk into her husband's room. "Excuse me."

Kristen watched the small woman follow the nurses inside. Less than a minute later, Aiden walked out of his father's room.

"Ready?" He took her hand and they started walking back toward the elevators. They rushed through the rain to his car. He opened her door and waited for her before running around and getting behind the wheel. "Sorry, I just had to get out of there." He turned toward her. "He started talking to me like I was five again."

"I'm sorry." She reached over and took his hand. He looked down at their joined fingers.

"I always thought it was Shannon keeping me from seeing him." He shook his head and she could see the pain in his eyes. "But all along it was him."

"Did he say why?"

"At first, he was busy with his career and making a life with Shannon, but then, when his health turned, he didn't want me to see him like that." He sighed and closed his eyes.

"Sometimes people do things to shelter the ones they love." She waited until he looked at her to finish. "Amy's parents have done some pretty stupid stuff in the last few years since their divorce."

She could see he was tired from the whole ordeal.

"How about some food? I know this great pizza place," he asked after a moment.

"As long as there's a cold beer next to it," she replied.

"Yeah, definitely in the mood for pizza and beer."

They drove to one of Kristen's favorite chain pizza places, Beau Jo's, and split a large pie between them. They drank cold beer as they watched the rainfall from the large windows.

"Why didn't you tell me who your father was?" she asked as she reached for her second slice of pie.

"I guess I never really think about it. I mean, he wasn't around all that much when I was a kid, and then he took off with my babysitter." He groaned and closed his eyes. She could tell the hurt and betrayal he felt was still raw. When he opened them, he reached for his beer and took a sip.

"That must have been hard."

He chuckled bitterly. "You know, the worst part was that Shannon was my first crush. Some guys have it for teachers; I had it for my babysitter." He shrugged and finished off his second piece of pie, then reached for another slice.

"My first crush was on my neighbor. I was going to marry him when I turned eight."

"Things didn't work out?" he joked.

"No, he had a thing for Jenny, down the block."

"His loss," he murmured. She smiled as he took her hand. "Thanks for being there today." He took her hand up to his lips and brushed a kiss across her knuckles. Her heart skipped a little at the gesture.

By the time they left the pizza place, the rain had stopped, leaving the streets looking clean. When he took her hand again and asked if she wanted to walk for a while, she nodded and pulled her jacket closer to her.

"It's amazing how chilly it gets up here at night," she said, feeling the bite of the mountain air on her face.

He wrapped his arm around her. "I went to the top of Pikes Peak one summer. It was a boiling ninety-something down in the Springs, but when I got to the top, it was snowing."

"Did you ride the train or drive up to the top?"

"Drove. I've always wanted to ride the train, though."

They walked by a few stores and even went in a couple of them. But mostly they walked and talked about some of the time he'd spent with his father in the mountains when he'd been a kid.

"How about heading over to the hotel and calling it a night?" He took her hand in his again.

"Sounds good." She tried to stifle a yawn. She'd gotten in late and had woken up early to get her work done. Not to mention that falling asleep had been extra hard, since all she could think about was having Aiden touch her again.

CHAPTER
TWELVE

Aiden stood back as he opened the door to their hotel room. He'd made a point to reserve one of the nicest suites at The Lodge in downtown Vail. During ski season, the place was packed, but the slopes were somewhat deserted thanks to the spring weather they'd had in the mountains, so the hotel looked fairly empty.

Their room was on the top floor, and he didn't doubt it would have a killer view of the mountains and ski slopes come morning.

"Wow, look at this," Kristen said, stepping into the room quickly. He walked into the room behind her and shut the door with his foot as he set their bags down just inside the doorway. He watched her as she moved around the large living area where a huge stone fireplace sat on one wall and a large sofa on the other. Then she disappeared down a short hallway toward the back room and he heard her gasp. When he followed her to the bedroom, he smiled. There was a king-size four-poster bed sitting in the corner of the room. There were large windows, and another stone fireplace sat on the wall opposite the bed.

He leaned against the doorframe as she walked around the room. When she went into the bathroom, he followed her more slowly.

He stepped into the bright room and instantly dreamed of pulling her into the large glass shower.

Their hotel room was bigger than her apartment, a fact that didn't go unnoticed by her.

She turned and looked at him. "Are you sure this is the right room?"

He moved closer to her. "You know, after such a long drive, I sure could use a hot shower." He nudged her jacket off her shoulders as he watched her bite her bottom lip. "You too."

"I was actually thinking about taking a long bubble bath." She nodded toward the large jet tub.

He smiled. "Shower tonight, bath in the morning?"

She shook her head and frowned a little. He watched the movement of her lips, and desire flooded his entire body. "Okay, bath tonight, shower in the morning."

Her eyes softened. "You read my mind."

His hands went to her hips as she started pulling the buttons of his shirt open slowly, one by one. When she ran her fingers over his bare chest, his nails dug into her soft hips. He felt himself grow so hard that he doubted he would be able to wait for the bath to fill up all the way.

"Kristen," he moaned against her lips. He felt her chuckle. "You think this is funny?" He moved back and looked down at her.

"You don't?" Her soft eyes laughed at him.

He smiled, then slowly removed her shirt. Her eyes heated as his fingers grazed her skin underneath.

"So beautiful," he moaned, running a finger down her shoulder. She swayed as she closed her eyes.

Just looking at her pale skin had his blood steaming. When her eyes opened again, he could see matching desire.

"Aiden?" She reached up and gripped his shoulders.

"Hmm?" He pulled on her hips until she fit tight against him.

"I don't think I can wait for the bath." Her fingernails dug into his muscles.

"No, neither can I." In one quick motion, he swooped her up into his arms. She sighed as he carried her out of the bathroom and laid her gently on the bed.

She unbuttoned her slacks, and he helped her pull them down her long legs. He paused to appreciate the view of her lying on the large bed in nothing but a matching pair of rose-colored silk undergarments, and he wished he could hold on to that memory for the rest of his life.

"If I were an artist, I'd paint you just like this." He stood over her and watched the smile form on her lips. Her soft hair was fanned out on the bedspread. The supple material had small green leaves on it that matched her eyes almost perfectly.

"Aiden." She reached up a hand and held it out to him. When he started to move toward her, his mind sharpened.

"Damn." He held up a finger. "Hang on just a moment." He rushed from the room and gathered their bags and brought them into the bedroom, then pulled out a few condoms. Taking one, he set the rest on the nightstand beside the bed.

"Ready?" she asked.

He watched her reach for the buckle of his jeans.

"Have I told you how much I love your body?" she asked, her eyes going to his as she ran her hands over his chest.

"Same here." His fingers skimmed her flat stomach and he watched her inhale as he touched a ticklish spot. He decided to save that knowledge for later and slid the straps of her bra down slowly.

She twitched and twisted under him as he used his fingertips to explore every inch of her. Finally, once she lay in front of him completely bare, he allowed her to tug off his boxer briefs. When he moved to slide on the condom, she took it from him and slid the protection on him slowly, inch by agonizing inch.

"You're killing me," he whispered.

"Good, now you know how I feel." She yanked on him until he moved over her. When she wrapped her legs around his hips, he slowly penetrated her heat.

Her shoulders jerked off the mattress as she moaned his name until he covered her mouth with his. Her tongue darted out, heating the kiss until he felt himself gasping for breath as his hips moved on their own accord.

He lost control when he felt her inner muscles convulse around him, holding him, begging him for more. When her legs and arms released him, he knew that she was spent, but still he demanded more.

He wanted to growl, to shout out his joy at giving her complete pleasure, but he was too focused on needing more from her.

"Again," he said next to her mouth. His hands clasped hers and carried them over her head as he raced faster, harder. His lips trailed down her neck, until his mouth clamped over her nipple. He moaned when he felt it pucker for him, and then he scraped his teeth lightly over the bud and felt her hips jerk in response. "Again," he repeated as he leaned over her and repeated his torture on her other breast.

"Aiden!" she cried out as he felt her legs wrap once more around his hips.

He continued the speed of his hips, pushing her faster as her body heated next to his. When he saw her eyes lock with his, he knew she was about to fall and willingly followed her to enjoy the sweet ending together.

◆ ◆ ◆

Kristen leaned back against Aiden's chest and let the bubbles and the warm water soak away the last aches in her body.

"Better?" She felt him ask as she heard the sound vibrating in his chest.

She nodded as his hands ran over the front of her body in a lazy motion. He had a washcloth full of soap, which was causing little bumps to rise all over her skin. But it felt too wonderful to move.

Her hair was wet and pushed to the side, and she felt his warm breath on her neck. She could stay like this forever. She sighed and closed her eyes.

"You were right," he said, moving just a little underneath her.

"Hmm?" She let her hands float in the water next to her. Her chest rose out of the bubbly water with every breath she took, but she didn't mind. Actually, the feeling of the motion caused her some pleasure.

"A bath was a better idea." He moved just a little more until she felt him against her back.

She couldn't stop the moan from escaping her lips as she felt him harden in the water. Images flooded her mind of making love to him in the large tub.

When she heard him unwrap another condom, she felt her heart kick a beat. Then the water sloshed around as he sheathed himself for her.

When his hands went to her hips, she let him guide her up until she felt the head of his erection at her entrance. She moaned as he released her and she slid slowly onto him.

"Yeah, I could definitely get used to taking a bath." His hands held her hips in place and she felt an urgent need to move. "That's it," he groaned. "My God," he said against her neck as he took her hands in his.

She leaned her head back against his chest as she moved over him. When she wanted more speed, she gripped her feet on the bottom of the tub and used her thigh muscles until they screamed. Then she pulled away and twisted toward him until she could straddle him in the tub. He sat forward a little, allowing her legs to wrap around him.

His mouth covered hers as she slid down on him again. This time, she rode him harder, faster, and the water threatened to slosh over the edge of the tub. Her fingers fisted in his hair, holding him still as she ran her mouth over him, dueling his tongue with her own.

His fingers dug into her hips and her butt as he helped her move over him. She felt herself building and wanted to make sure he followed her.

"Please," she begged as she felt herself starting to let go. He reached up and wrapped his arms around her waist, holding her close as his mouth took hers in a kiss that was deeper than any she'd experienced before.

When she finally heard him growl out her name, she smiled in victory and followed him over the edge.

"I'm glad we didn't try that in the shower," he said a few minutes later after they'd pulled themselves out of the water and dried off.

She chuckled and, wrapped only in a large, soft towel, flung herself on the bed.

She watched him set his cell phone on the nightstand and rolled over to her side and propped her head on her arm, watching him move around the room.

"We'll need to head out pretty early," Aiden said. She guessed he needed to chat to keep his mind busy, so she leaned back and listened to him talk about tomorrow's plans. "I wanted to swing by the hospital once more before we head back down the mountain," he said, and she could tell he was beginning to think about his father again.

"Are you going to tell me what happened between you and your father at the hospital?" she asked.

He frowned, then walked over and sat next to her.

"There really isn't that much to tell. He was lucid for a little while." He closed his eyes briefly. "After you left the room, he started talking to me like I was five again." He exhaled sharply. "I didn't know."

"My grandfather had Alzheimer's." She reached out and took his hand and squeezed it lightly. "My grandmother finally had to put him in a home a few years back." She moved over as he climbed in beside her. The white towel that he'd wrapped around his waist loosened a little and he tucked it closer. "He pretty much functioned right up until that point. Then he started taking walks and getting lost. He almost burned their house down when he tried to make French toast one morning. That's when we decided it was best for his safety to move him into a home where he could be watched more closely."

He took her hands in his, looking down at them as he spoke. "I don't know how far gone he is yet. He told me he'd been diagnosed almost four years ago."

She could see the hurt in his eyes.

"I had been led, all this time, to believe it was Shannon who had kept me away from my father." He moaned and pulled her closer. She rested her head against his warm chest and wrapped her arms around him. "I never thought he was the one. I mean, he'd been an okay dad. Not that he would have earned any father-of-the-year awards, but he hadn't been bad. When my parents first divorced, I saw him every other weekend. That was until he married Shannon a little over a year later." He absently rubbed his hands through her wet hair. If she could, she would have purred. "Then I started seeing him less and less. When Mom and Eric got married, it slowed down to only during the holidays. I thought it was because he was trying to give them space, you know. When Ashley had been born, I felt outnumbered by the girls in the house and asked if I could move in with him. But Shannon called me up and told me that it wouldn't work, since they were moving to the mountains."

"I'm sure they had their reasons for moving," she said, running her finger over his chest.

"Yeah, Dad had just retired and Shannon had gotten a job in Vail as a realtor. Anyway, after that, every chance I could get to the mountains, I would try to see him. In ten years, I think I only saw him two times. The last time he pulled his shotgun on me and told me to get off his property. Now I know why."

"Alzheimer's is hard. Especially on the loved ones. I think my grandmother struggles more than my grandfather does." She sighed. "Half the time, he thinks he's at a resort in the Bahamas." She glanced up at him but her smile fell away when she noticed the sadness still in his eyes. "My grandmother visits every day. On a good day, he recognizes her."

"I'm glad you came with me today." He rubbed his hand over her hair again.

"Me too," she said, wrapping her arms around him.

CHAPTER THIRTEEN

Aiden lay in the dark with Kristen wrapped around him and couldn't shut down his mind. Even though his body was completely sated from the hours of making love to Kristen, his mind refused to let him rest. So, he held her as she slept blissfully through the night, and he thought about his father.

It had been a hard blow, hearing of his stroke, but Alzheimer's on top of it all was almost too much. He wanted to call his mom and find out if she had known about it. Something told him that she had been hiding it from him for a while.

He rubbed a lock of Kristen's hair between his fingertips. He could feel her naked body pressed up next to his. Every breath she took was pure heaven as her skin brushed against his.

He'd never thought he could get this close to someone so fast. Especially since his track record wasn't all that impressive. He almost chuckled out loud when he remembered Kristen's history of relationships. How is it that a woman of her caliber had such terrible luck when it came to men?

He felt her shift in her sleep and pulled her closer, wrapping his arm more tightly around her. She felt good in his arms. Right somehow. He closed his eyes, remembering their evening together, how she'd matched his every move, pace for pace.

He knew he'd been with more sexual partners than she had, but honestly, he could say he'd never had what they had together. Never.

He finally drifted off, his mind filled with Kristen as sleep finally overtook him.

When he woke in the morning, his arms were empty so he felt around the large bed for her. The sheets and pillowcase were cold next to him, telling him that she'd gotten up some time before.

When he finally cracked open his eyes, he immediately shut them again. The room was too bright. Rolling over, he squinted and glanced at the windows. The curtains, which had been closed last night, were thrown back wide. He groaned and rolled over toward the bathroom, hoping to hear the shower running. He frowned when he couldn't hear a sound coming from the bathroom.

Standing up, he stretched his arms over his head and rolled the kinks out of his neck caused by sleeping in the same spot as he held Kristen. He would gladly wake up with a sore neck every morning as long as she lay next to him like she had last night.

He walked into the bathroom and when he walked out, Kristen was sitting on the edge of the bed, looking down at her phone. When she heard him walk in, she looked up at him and smiled. He watched her smile falter when she realized he was still completely naked.

"You did promise me a shower this morning." He walked over to her and pulled her up off the bed. She had tossed on a pair of jeans and a T-shirt. He could tell she hadn't showered, since her hair was completely dry.

"I guess I did." She wrapped her arms around his shoulders as he started walking backward toward the bathroom. When he dipped his head down and placed a soft kiss on her lips, he knew he was officially in trouble. His heart almost beat out of his chest and he felt his legs go wobbly underneath him. Instead of freaking out, he decided to grab hold and enjoy the ride.

An hour later, he stood in the bedroom waiting for her to finish drying her hair. He'd carried his bag down to the trunk of his car and was dealing with a few e-mails on his phone as he waited.

He'd called and left a message for his mom, but he knew she and Eric were probably already at church.

"We can grab some breakfast at the coffee shop downstairs on our way out," he yelled over her blow-dryer.

"Sounds good. For some reason, I'm starving." She smiled over at him as she brushed through her hair. "All done." She turned off the hair dryer.

"I figured we'd make it back downtown in time to hit a couple furniture stores." He walked over and leaned on the counter next to her. She frowned and he saw something cross her eyes.

"What?" His eyebrows pulled together.

"It's nothing, really." She bent down and zipped the bag shut.

"Kristen." He waited until she stood up again, then took her shoulders and held her still. "I saw that look. What's wrong with us going shopping for a bed and sofa for you?"

"Nothing, really. It's just, last time I was at a furniture store, I found out my boyfriend had a wife and kids." She sighed. "I guess it kind of spoiled shopping for a sofa for me. Kind of like how getting carjacked ruined buying a new car."

He shook his head and then pulled her face up until their eyes met. "Is this why you still don't have any furniture?"

"I guess so. I just can't bring myself to step foot in a furniture store again."

"Well, that's because you haven't gone with me." He leaned in and quickly kissed her, then dipped down and picked up her bag. "Got everything?"

She looked around and nodded. "Yes, everything."

"Did you see the view from the living room?" he asked as they were walking by.

She gasped and walked over to the windows. He was right; the view was spectacular. "Yeah, a person could get used to that," she said.

He had stopped and followed her to the windows to pull her close for just a moment.

"Come winter, I don't know if I could deal with being snowed in, though." She sighed, feeling wonderful in his arms.

"I bet we could find something to keep your mind off being snowed in," he said, smiling into her hair.

She chuckled and reached up to kiss him.

After eating warm blueberry muffins and having cups of coffee, they swung by the hospital one last time.

This time, the visit was more for Shannon than his father, who was not having a good day. It was hard when the old man didn't recognize him at all today. He actually thought he was a doctor, come to check up on him.

When they walked in, he asked Shannon if he could talk to her for a moment. She nodded, not saying anything, but followed him to the doorway.

"I want to apologize." He pulled Shannon closer to the doorway. "I haven't always treated you—"

"No, let me first. I wanted to tell you about your father, but . . ." She looked over to the man who was sitting up in bed watching television. "Gordon can be stubborn."

He leaned down and kissed her on her cheek. "You're too good for him. I'm sorry."

"It was nice of you to drive up here." She leaned in. "I like your girl, Kristen," she whispered.

"Me too." Then he hugged her before he turned and walked out with Kristen.

The drive down the mountain was always peaceful. Even when large semis slowed the right lanes down at the steepest parts, his car hugged the roads and he enjoyed the drive. Kristen looked comfortable enough as they took the last hill and Denver came into view.

"This is my favorite view of the city," he said. She sighed and leaned forward to get a better look out his windshield. "This and the view at Red Rocks." He glanced at her.

"I love Red Rocks." She smiled. "I can't tell you how many concerts Amy and I have been to there." She giggled. "Since we lived so close, we used to bike there during the day when we were teenagers." She leaned back in the seat and he watched her eyes go almost misty with memories.

"I figured we'd hit a few furniture stores downtown first. I have a friend who owns Albert's."

"Really?" She turned toward him.

"Went to high school with him. He took over the shop when his grandfather passed away a few years back."

"I've used Albert's lots of times for some of our higher-paying clients." She frowned. "But, I don't think I can . . ."

He stopped her by taking her hand. "Tom owes me a favor. I'm sure he will have something that will work."

◆　◆　◆

Kristen sighed as she dreamed about the soft cream-colored sofa that sat in front of her. But her insurance check wasn't enough to buy a doorstop in a place like this, let alone a name-brand, top-of-the-line, one-of-a-kind, soft leather sofa.

She knew that even just dreaming about buying furniture from Albert's was probably costing her too much.

Aiden walked over to her and smiled. "That's a beauty." He sat down on the plush leather. She'd tested it out herself just a minute ago. So far, it was the most comfortable sofa she'd ever sat on and she desperately wanted it. But the insurance check also had to cover a new bed, nightstands, a dresser, and a table and chairs for her dining room.

This sofa was out of her league.

"Oh! Come try it out." He patted the spot next to him. He was like a kid in a candy store. Ever since they walked through the front doors less than half an hour ago, he'd been sitting on every sofa, lying on every mattress, and opening every drawer on the dressers.

She moved over and sat next to him. The sofa was better the second time around. She leaned back into the crook of his arm and relaxed.

"It's lovely, but with a price tag like that"—she pointed to the yellow tag hanging off the corner—"I'm better off sticking with my beanbags."

"There he is now . . ." He nodded toward a tall blond man that was walking their way. His hair was a little long and had a slight curl to it. He looked around their age, and when he approached them, Aiden stood up and gave the man a hug.

"Tom, this is Kristen. Kristen, Tom." Aiden stood back so she could shake the man's hand.

Tom's eyes ran up and down her, and for a moment, she thought he was going to hug her as well. Then he shook her hand and turned back toward Aiden. "I see you're keeping yourself busy."

Aiden turned to her and sobered a little. "Kristen lost all her furniture a while back."

Tom's eyebrows shot up in question. "Fire?"

She shook her head. "Thieving ex-boyfriend."

He laughed quickly, the sound vibrating in the large room, then he took her hand in his and stood close to her. "My dear, we're here to please. What do you think of the Lexington?" He pointed to the cream sofa of her dreams.

She glanced back down at the perfect sofa. "It's lovely. Too bad it comes with such a big price tag."

Tom smiled at her and his blue eyes were mesmerizing. She blinked a few times and then looked over at Aiden's darker ones. Aiden was looking at her, and when their eyes met, she felt the heat of his gaze singe her down to her toes.

Who would have thought that Aiden's brown eyes and crooked smile could make her knees go weak from a few feet away? Especially while Adonis was holding her hand.

"Well, I think there's something I can do about that." Tom smiled and she noticed how perfect his teeth were. Funny, a few months ago she would have swooned over the man, but now she was thinking how perfect another less-than-straight smile was.

Tom dropped her hand and walked over to the tag, then ripped it off and tore it up. "Any friend of Aiden's is a friend of mine. Let's head to my office and talk about what else you need." He took her arm again and started walking toward the stairs. She glanced back and watched Aiden following them. When he saw her look, he winked at her.

Less than an hour later, they walked out of the store. She was now the proud owner of not only the cream-colored Lexington sofa but a gorgeous queen-sized cherry bed frame with a matching dresser and nightstands, and a pillow-top mattress to boot. Not to mention that she would still have money left over to buy a dining room set. Everything was going to be delivered to her apartment later that week.

"Man, Tom must owe you big time," she said after Aiden got into the car and started it up.

He nodded. "Yeah. That will teach him to flirt with my sister ever again."

Kristen smiled. "Which one? Amber or Ashley?"

He looked at her. "Amber. Ashley is only eighteen. If I had caught him trying to kiss Ashley he would have had to give you everything in the store." He frowned as she laughed.

"He does have flirting down to a science." She reached over and took his hand as he drove. He smiled at her. "You know . . ." She watched him closely. "A few months ago, I would have fallen for his tricks."

He glanced at her, his eyebrows shooting up. "Tom? Tom's your type?" He laughed. The rich sound filled his small car. She couldn't help it—she smiled hearing it.

"Tall, blonde, blue-eyed, beach-bum look." She sighed. "Adonis in a suit."

His smile fell away a little. "Seriously?"

She dropped his hand and crossed her arms over her chest.

"What's wrong with the type?" she asked.

"Up until a while ago, you would have seen me with a tall, blonde, blue-eyed woman who looked like she'd been on the cover of at least one magazine."

She hid her frown. She didn't mind being honest with him, but for some reason, she hadn't expected his honesty to sting so much.

He reached over and took her hand again. "Hey, but now I can't even imagine spending my time with anyone other than you."

She beamed. "I feel the same way." Even though she'd said it, for some reason just the thought of him with a woman like that hurt.

She knew she wasn't much to look at. Her caramel-colored hair was plain, and it frizzed every time it snowed or rained. Her green eyes were her best feature, if anyone could get close enough to see them. She'd worked hard on keeping her body toned. Of course, it helped that she walked a lot every day.

Still, she sat quietly thinking the entire way back to her place. When he parked out front of her apartment, he leaned over and pulled her close.

"Pack a bag and come stay with me. At least until your furniture arrives," he said between kisses.

There was too much for her to think about, and she doubted she could do it with him around. She needed some time inside her own head, to better understand all the new feelings she was having. She couldn't explain it, but this relationship was far different than any she'd ever been in before. It mattered more to her that she try to understand why that was.

"I . . ." She couldn't think of a reason, so instead she just shook her head. "I'd better go. Thanks."

He jumped out of the car and rushed to the trunk and pulled out her bag. When he handed it to her, she was thankful that he hadn't argued or demanded a reason. "I'll see you tomorrow." He pulled her closer and kissed her until she questioned why she was heading up to her apartment alone instead of going back to his place and having hot monkey sex all night.

When she closed her front door behind her, she rested on the cool wood and closed her eyes. How had she ended up falling for someone like Aiden so quickly?

CHAPTER
FOURTEEN

The next week was a very busy one for Aiden. Several times during his workday at R&S, he had to take calls or deal with his own business. Once, he had to ride the bus down to his office and spend his entire lunch break in a meeting with one of his own clients. He had really wanted to spend that lunch time with Kristen instead.

Even though he had a car sitting in the garage, he really enjoyed riding the bus back and forth to the office. He supposed he was doing his part to cut down on emissions. But in truth, he really liked people watching. It helped clear his head and gave him something else to focus on other than work, or Kristen.

He had pulled Kristen into his office several times, but since there was a large window in his half wall, he hadn't been able to touch her. Instead, he'd talked to her and told her exactly what he wanted to do with her. He'd watched her eyes heat and seen her face flush, causing him to become even more aroused.

He had gotten a few minutes of alone time with her when he'd pulled her into Darren's small office. He knew that the IT guy had been working in the conference room on the projector. He'd held on to her in the dark office and covered her mouth with a hungry kiss as his hands had roamed over every inch of her he could expose. By the time he let her go, she'd cried out his name and he'd had to help her make sure her clothes were back to normal. He'd even had to help her re-pile her hair on the top of her head in a bun. As she'd walked away, he'd tried not to laugh, knowing that if she bumped into anyone in the next five minutes, they would know exactly what she'd been doing.

The rest of the week flew by. He wasn't complaining, but he'd really hoped to have more time with Kristen. As it was, she'd been out to the Market Place site several days. By Friday, he was jonesing for some more time alone with her.

She'd talked to him on the phone the entire time the guys were delivering her new furniture. He'd wanted to head over there to help her, but he'd been tied up with a few meetings that couldn't be rescheduled.

She had understood and told him that Amy had helped her set everything up anyway. Then she'd shown him pictures of the place on her phone the next day. Still, he couldn't wait to see it for himself.

The weather had turned warmer and he could tell spring was in full season. He'd had a long talk with his mother and Eric and had listened to her explain why she'd kept his father's recent condition from him. How she had tried to save him from knowing that his father was slowly going crazy the last few years. And, more importantly, why his father had decided to focus on his career instead of raising his son.

Even though he'd tried to understand why his mom had tried to shield him, part of him was still very upset that she hadn't told him earlier. She'd begged him to forgive her and understand, but he still felt there was a rift between them that hadn't been there before. She'd asked to see him so they could talk it over, but he'd told her his schedule had been booked solid.

His mother even had Amber call him to try to convince him to meet with their mom, which was a very low blow considering he could never deny his sister anything.

By the end of their conversation, he'd agreed to a family lunch that weekend, and even promised, without Kristen's knowledge, that he'd bring her. Now he just had to convince Kristen to go along with him.

It was Friday evening and he'd arranged to meet Kristen back at the office since she'd had another late appointment at Market Place. They were going to head over to her place to meet Amy for dinner.

He swung by the R&S office after his own appointment to handle a few items. When he entered the building, most of the lights were off since it was a quarter after six.

As he started walking toward the row of elevators, he heard the alarm buzzing in one of them. Looking around and seeing no one, he punched the button several times.

"Hello?" he called out, knowing that it would be almost impossible for anyone stuck in the elevator to hear him. Especially if they were on one of the higher floors.

Two elevators out of the four came down and opened for him. He walked into one of them and picked up the phone.

"Security." The voice was garbled and hard to hear.

"Yes, this is Aiden Scott with Row and Stein. Someone has set off an alarm in one of the west side elevators."

"Yes, Mr. Scott. We are aware of the issue. Help is on the way." The man sounded bored.

"Um, okay. Is someone locked in there?"

"Not that we know. The emergency phone isn't working in that unit. We've called in the repairman and he'll be there within the hour."

Spending an hour in a locked elevator was not his idea of a fun way to spend a Friday night. Aiden hung up the phone and punched his floor.

When the doors opened, he could still hear the alarm ringing. He walked into the office and frowned. It was too dark for Kristen to still be here. As he walked by the balcony, he glanced outside, just in case.

Then his heart caught in his chest. He rushed toward her cubicle, and when he noticed it was empty, he rushed back outside to the elevators.

"Kristen?" he called loudly several times. Then he stopped and put his ear to the metal doors and heard the whimper.

◆ ◆ ◆

Kristen tried to keep it together. But after the first ten minutes, time seemed to slow down. Her watch face blurred as tears formed in her eyes. Her breath hitched as she walked back and forth trying to think of a million things other than the fact that she was locked in a five-by-five space and her air was quickly running out.

Well, okay, maybe she wouldn't suffocate, but she was definitely going to hyperventilate. What had she done in life to deserve this? Certainly, it couldn't be just because she'd gone out with a boy on his sister's birthday. She stomped her foot lightly as she crossed her arms over her chest. When she felt the elevator shake a little, she quickly grabbed hold of the rail and closed her eyes.

"Okay, I won't be doing that again." She prayed silently that someone would come soon. The loud alarm was giving her a headache, but since there was no way of turning it off herself, she had to listen to the buzzing until someone rescued her. She'd tried her cell phone, but with zero bars, she doubted it would be any help. She was able, however, to send out a few text messages. The first one was to Amy, telling her quickly of her situation. The second had been to Aiden, asking if he was in the building. She didn't want to tell him what was going on. It all seemed too embarrassing to admit to him just yet, at least until she could control her panicked state.

She rested her head on the cool, mirrored wall and tried to count the rapid heartbeats pounding in her head to steady herself. When that didn't help, she let her mind drift to last weekend. How wonderful it had been being with Aiden in Vail. He'd been a perfect dream guy. Was he too perfect?

After everything she'd been through in the past few months, could she really trust someone like him? Did she want to put her heart on the line? Could she afford to?

Just then she heard someone calling her name. Looking up, she heard it again. A cry of relief escaped her lips.

"Here! I'm here!" she called out over and over again. Her knees shook so she gripped the handle harder.

"I'm calling security again." Aiden's muffled call was music to her ears. She waited, but the shaking in her knees grew with every passing minute. Her ears were ringing loudly. She couldn't hear him anymore.

Finally, she heard him yell down, "Kristen, help is on the way. Are you okay?"

"Yes," she called back. "Just scared out of my mind." She whispered the last part under her breath as she looked around her mirror-walled prison. Seeing her own scared face staring back at her, she moaned and shook her head clear. "You haven't done anything to deserve this. Aiden's right. You make your own luck." She promised her reflection she'd make better judgments in the future. She'd known this elevator sometimes had issues. She should have waited for the next one instead of hopping on it because she'd been too focused on rushing upstairs.

"Can you tell me how far away you are from our floor?" he called out again.

She closed her eyes, trying to remember how many floors she'd gone up before the digital display had shut off. "I think I'm on six," she called out.

"Okay, I'm going to run down the stairs toward you. I'll be right back."

She leaned against the wall. With every movement she made, the cart jiggled and swayed. She hated elevators.

"Kristen?" Aiden's voice was much closer now.

"Yes." She took a deep breath, praying that this would all be over soon.

"I'm here," he said through the door.

She took a small step toward the mirrored exit.

"I think something's wrong. I mean, the elevator shakes really bad every time I move. When it stopped"—she took another small step toward the doors—"it jolted and I thought I heard something snap." She looked down at her hands and knees, thinking about the pain she'd felt when she'd fallen on them as the elevator jolted to a stop the first time. Now, everything was dull since her heartbeat was going nuts.

"Damn." She heard him moving around. He did something that caused the whole box to shake.

"Aiden! Stop!" she screamed and felt tears sliding down her face. She'd fallen to her knees again. When she opened her eyes, she was looking down at her hands, which were spread out on the floor. "Please," she said under her breath.

"Kristen?" She could hear him screaming her name over again. "I'm sorry, baby. I'm just trying to get the doors open." She could hear the strain in his voice. "I need to make a call. Don't move, okay?"

"I'm not going anywhere." She added *I hope* in her mind.

She could hear him cussing and yelling at someone, most likely security on another elevator's phone. This one hadn't worked. She looked up and glared at the silver box that had a black phone hanging out of it.

"If I didn't know better, I'd say you have it out for me." She blinked and tried to focus on Aiden's voice. She could hear him arguing with someone else. Then he came back to her and she focused on how great his voice sounded.

"Kristen, the fire department is on their way up here. Just hold on." She could hear the worry in his voice.

"Kristen?" he called out again.

"Yes, I'm all right." She kept her eyes closed and continued to pray. Her fingernails dug into her skin as she fisted her hands tightly. Images of a thin wire holding up the elevator car flashed through her mind.

Aiden continued to talk to her until she heard other voices, then there was a bunch of noise and the car bumped around even more. She thought she had screamed, but she couldn't be sure since all she could hear was the blood pounding in her ears.

She stayed on her hands and knees, she could hear her breath whooshing out quickly, then she heard Aiden's voice just above her. When she looked up, she could see his face poking through the doors, which were being held open by two large firemen.

"Babe, you have to come to me," he was saying. "Crawl over to the door and then stand up and reach for my hand."

"Can't." It came out as a whisper.

"Sure you can. They've secured the car, it's not going anywhere."

Even this knowledge didn't comfort her. Her mind was too preoccupied with images of it and her speeding down flight after flight and crashing at the bottom.

"Kristen." He held out his hand. "Come here. You can do it."

She took a deep breath and then looked back down at her hands. Two of her nails were chipped. The bright pink nail polish she'd let Amy put on her the other night was no longer pretty and perfect. She could just imagine how she'd look after falling almost a dozen floors to the bottom floor in the parking garage.

"I can't move," she said softly.

"Hang on! I'm coming down to you," he said and she could hear him moving around.

"No!" She looked up quickly. She didn't want him to put himself in danger because of her. "I'll . . . I'm coming to you."

She forced herself to move. It was slow going, but she crawled her way toward the doors, braced herself up against the mirrored wall, and pulled herself up until she felt her knees almost give out.

Her hand touched Aiden's warmer one and she felt her breath whoosh out of her as she was grabbed under her arms and hoisted up into midair. She kept her eyes shut until she felt Aiden's arms around her, holding her tight.

Instantly she felt safe. All the darkness and fear dissipated as he held her against his chest. She had never felt like this with a man before and wondered if she'd gone a little mad locked in the elevator.

CHAPTER
FIFTEEN

Aiden didn't want to let go of her. When he'd first seen her sitting on the floor of the elevator, she had been so pale and looked utterly scared. Instantly his heart had broken.

Now, as he held her and kissed the top of her head, he could feel her shake and her knees give out on her. The firemen who'd helped him pry open the doors and secure the car stood around him, trying to look busy.

"Miss, do you need any medical help?" one of them finally said.

She shook her head between sobs. Aiden answered for her since she hadn't been able to speak. "I think she's just shaken up," he said, then leaned back and took her face in his hands. "Are you okay to head downstairs?"

"Maybe"—she shook a little more—"if I had a moment . . ." She nodded to the left where the bathrooms were.

He smiled. "I'll be right here."

She moved slowly. "My stuff . . ." She pointed toward the elevator.

"They'll get it out for you by the time you're done in there." He could see a fireman and an electrician had already jumped into the elevator car and were working on the electrical console.

When Kristen disappeared into the bathroom, he walked over and gathered her laptop bag, her design case, and her small purse. Her cell phone was tucked in the side pocket of her purse, and the second he walked toward the stairs, it started ringing.

Looking down, he saw a picture of a pretty blonde smiling back at him with Amy written across the screen.

He punched the button. "Hello?"

"Who is this? Is Kristen okay? I got a bunch of text messages . . ."

"This is Aiden Scott. Yes, she's okay. She's out of the elevator," he said. "She's just in the restroom." He turned and looked toward the closed door.

"What happened?" He could hear the concern in her friend's voice.

"It appears that one of the cables in the elevator snapped, causing the brakes to lock."

"Oh my God! It didn't fall with her in it, did it?"

"No. They tell me it would have only gone a few feet before the locks engaged."

He heard the woman sigh. "She didn't get hurt?"

"No, just shaken. I'll bring her back to her place since we were supposed to meet you there." He turned when he heard Kristen walk out of the bathroom. She'd splashed some water on her face and had pushed her hair back. He could see her eyes were wet and red, but she was looking a lot more together than she had before. "Here she is now." He held out the phone for her. "Amy."

She reached for the phone and he noticed that her hands still shook.

"I'm okay." She walked back into his arms, which he held open for her. "I'm with Aiden now," she said with her face pressed against his chest.

He listened halfheartedly as she answered more of Amy's questions.

"We should be there in about half an hour." She sighed. "Okay, thanks."

She hung up and looked up at him. "I'd better call my folks since Amy called them panicking when she couldn't get ahold of me." He nodded and she stepped away from him to make the call.

After Kristen had assured her parents that she was alive and well, and after she and Aiden had talked to the firemen and the building manager, they took the stairs to the parking garage where his car was.

"I guess I'll add stairs to my workout," she said, after climbing in and leaning back in the seat.

"You can't run and hide from everything." He reached across the seat and brushed her hair behind her ear, then ran a finger down her cheek.

Her green eyes opened and zeroed in on him. "That's easy for you to say. You didn't spend an hour trapped ten floors up, dangling by a thread."

He laughed. "A little exaggeration never hurt anyone." His eyebrows went up.

"Well, okay, maybe not by a thread." She smiled.

He leaned over and took her lips once more in a kiss that assured him she was alive and well. By the time he pulled back, he felt a little unsteady and shaky.

"I'm in the mood for pizza," she blurted out. He could tell she was trying to lighten the mood, so he just nodded in agreement.

"I know just the place." He pulled out of the parking garage and headed toward her apartment.

"I'll want a quick shower. I'm sure Amy can keep you entertained until I'm done." She glanced over at him and his nerves jumped with her warm look.

When they pulled into her apartment complex, the pretty blonde from Kristen's phone was leaning against a Jeep right next to the parking spot he used.

Before he could turn off the engine, she was yanking Kristen's side door open. By the time he walked around the car, the two friends were in an unbreakable hug, crying in each other's arms.

Finally, Amy pulled back and glanced over at him. "Hi."

"Oh!" Kristen wiped away a few tears. "Amy, this is Aiden. Aiden, Amy Walker."

He reached out and shook her hand as her eyes ran up and down him several times.

"I'm going to hit the shower," Kristen said, tugging Amy along with her as they started to take the stairs toward her apartment. "Amy, can you keep Aiden company?"

"Sure." Amy glanced over her shoulder at him and he got the impression that he was going to be grilled the entire time.

When Kristen disappeared into the back, Amy sat on the new cream-colored sofa and looked up at him.

"Don't take this the wrong way, but I like you." She twisted her watch around her wrist as she smiled at him.

He almost tripped on the new rug Kristen had put down under a new coffee table. He wondered where and when she'd gotten it.

"You . . . do?" he asked, walking over and taking a seat next to her.

"I've seen the kind of guys Krissy attracts." She leaned back and turned toward him.

He liked the nickname and decided he might use it himself. "And?" He leaned back along with her.

"You're nothing like them. Dark hair, broody eyes, strong chin." Her eyes ran over him. "Expensive suit."

He looked down and frowned. "I didn't have time to change after my last meeting."

She bit her lip. "The only thing I can't figure out is . . ."

He waited as she squinted her eyes and ran them over him again. "What you're doing at R&S."

He felt his pulse kick. "Helping a friend out."

Her eyes scanned his. "Krissy told me about your connection with Paul and Steven. But something just isn't adding up."

He tilted his head. "What is it, exactly, that you do?"

She blinked a few times. "Real estate."

He remembered now. "If Kristen asked you to drop everything and help her with a job, would you?"

She nodded without hesitation. "You bet your tight little butt I would."

"My stepfather and Steven are as close as you and Kristen. So, when he called me, I jumped."

"Yes, but what exactly are you doing for them?" He was saved from answering when Kristen walked out, freshly showered and dressed in a long flowing cream skirt and a purple sweater.

"How are you feeling?" Amy jumped up from the sofa.

"Better." Her hair was still a little wet. Half of it was piled up on the top of her head, while the other half fell around her face in tight little curls. She had applied some makeup, and as far as he could tell, all the paleness was gone.

He got up, walked over to her, and wrapped her in his arms again. "You look lovely." He leaned down and kissed her, right in front of Amy.

"Jeez, get a room," she joked behind Kristen's back.

Kristen laughed. "You know, if you weren't here, I have a perfectly good one with a brand-new bed just a few feet away."

"Oh no." Amy walked over and pulled her from his arms. "I'm starving and I want to hear all about your ordeal in the elevator." She tugged Kristen toward the door. "Were there any cute firemen?" he heard her ask as they stepped outside.

◆　◆　◆

Kristen filled Amy in all the way through dinner. It wasn't as if she could avoid it, since Amy was asking so many questions. Aiden even got into it and answered every question she asked about what had taken place.

By the time their two pizzas were finished, Amy had finally run out of questions and the two friends had moved on to talking about the trip to Vail. By the time they had climbed back into the car, Amy had even moved on beyond that conversation. Kristen could tell her friend was trying to get as much information from Aiden as possible.

"So, who's this friend that owns Albert's?" She leaned forward in the backseat of Aiden's car as they drove back to her place.

"He's just my type," Kristen said, looking over at Aiden as he drove. When he smiled and looked over at her, she winked at their joke.

"Oh." Amy puckered up her lips. "Then never mind. So, Aiden, you don't happen to have any brothers?"

"Nope, two sisters." He glanced at her in the rearview mirror. "Sorry."

"I suppose it was too much to ask." She tapped Kristen on the shoulder. "If you decide it's not going to work out . . ."

"Jeez." She looked back at her friend. "You're being a little forward, aren't you?"

"Oh, Aiden knows I'm just having fun." She smiled at him, showing off the small dimples by her mouth. Kristen had always been jealous of her friend's dimples. Most girlfriends would want Amy's long blonde hair or her silver-blue eyes or her perfect little body, but no, Kristen had always wanted her dimples.

"Sure I do." He winked at her in the mirror. "But I don't think I'll be done with Kristen for a very long time." He reached over to take her hand. She sighed and heard a matching sigh from the backseat.

Okay, so he'd won over her best friend, a feat that no other man she'd ever dated had accomplished. Next up, her parents. She cringed when she thought of that meeting.

"Before I forget . . ." He turned to her. "Mom and Eric want to have us over this weekend. They want to thank you for going with me to Vail."

She almost chuckled. He must have been reading her mind. "Um, sure. What day?"

He glanced at her. "Are you sure?"

She nodded.

"Um, tomorrow . . . Saturday night."

She added, "As long as we can have Sunday brunch at my folks."

"Sounds like a plan."

When they drove up to her apartment, Amy instantly made an excuse to leave. Kristen really loved her friend.

"Would you like some coffee?" she asked as she stepped up the first stair.

"There was nothing you could say or do to stop me from coming upstairs," he whispered and pulled her close. She loved that she was almost as tall as him, standing this way. She wrapped her arms around his shoulders and kissed him.

"Good, because I'd hate to have to hit you over the head and drag you up these stairs," she said as he laughed.

She took his hand in hers and walked up the rest of the stairs quickly. Once inside, she was pleased when he pushed her back against the closed door. His mouth fused to hers as his hands roamed over her.

When he started tugging her clothes off, she pulled at his. Clothes hit the ground, and hands moved against skin as they fought to get each other naked.

When his hands roamed over her body, she winced at the pain. He jumped back like he'd been shot, his eyes moving over her entire body. She was leaning against the front door, gasping for breath as he looked at her.

"What the . . ." He frowned. "Damn it." He reached over and flipped on the overhead light. Then he was leaning down in front of her as he pulled up one of her legs and looked at the scrapes and large bruises that had formed when she had fallen in the elevator.

"You should have gotten medical attention." He glanced up at her.

"For some bruises?" She looked down and held back a gasp when she noticed how dark both of her knees were.

"You could have broken your kneecaps," he said as he reached up and looked at her elbows and hands. They weren't as bad as her knees and she was thankful that his eyes went back downward as he dropped her arms.

"I'm okay." She pushed her hands through his hair. "Really."

He looked up at her, and his frown softened a little. "You should put some ice on these."

She tugged on his hair until he stood up, his arms wrapping around her. "What I need right now is to finish what we started." She pulled him back to her.

When his mouth fell back on hers, she felt his hesitation, but then she nibbled on his lower lip until he moaned. She felt him harden again against her hip and pushed on his shoulders until he was up against the wall.

She finished tugging his boxer shorts down and then ran her hands slowly toward the sexy dark V that led her downward.

Her mouth trailed along the pathway her hands had just taken as his hands buried into her hair.

"Krissy," he moaned. She smiled at his use of her nickname.

"Yes?" she teased.

"Don't torture me." His dark eyes found hers and she could see the heat in them.

"Why not?" she asked before running her tongue over the length of him. His cock jumped toward her so she did it again.

"You're going to get it," he warned.

"Promises, promises." She took him all the way into her mouth. As her lips moved up and down on him, his fingers dug into her hair, holding, pushing. She didn't care.

He was beautiful and felt like silk in her mouth. She couldn't get enough of him. His soft moans and pleas were only exciting her further.

Finally, she felt him tense and thought he was almost finished, but his hands went under her arms and he hoisted her up and carried her a few feet to her new, soft sofa.

Then he yanked her panties aside, ripping them at the hip as his mouth covered her in a powerful kiss. She jolted with the unexpected flash of desire that pulsed through her. His name was ripped from her lips as his tongue darted in and out of her quickly. His fingers rolled her tight, sensitive bud, pinching it and rolling it until she felt she couldn't hold back any longer.

"Come for me," he moaned.

She shook her head back and forth. "No, you wouldn't for me." She glanced at him and dared him to force it from her.

He watched her, his lips curling up in a wicked smile. "You can't keep this from me." He bent and slid a finger into her heat as he nibbled on her bud.

He was right; there was no way she could have denied his wishes. Not when he was so efficient at the torture. Her shoulders came off the soft leather and her fingernails dug into his scalp as she cried out.

CHAPTER
SIXTEEN

When he felt Kristen's body go lax, he gently picked her up in his arms and carried her into her new queen bed. As he laid her down, he opened a condom and quickly put it on.

Instead of moving to her, he stood over her and just looked at her. She was more than he'd ever dreamed. Her beauty was beyond words. Internally and externally. He'd never felt this way for someone before. He thought about how loyal she was to her friends. A twinge of guilt hit him about keeping secrets from her.

"Aiden?" She held out her hands for him, breaking him from his thoughts. He smiled and realized there was no way he would deny her anything. How had he fallen so quickly?

All questions and doubt exited his mind the second he slid into her. She was perfect. She was home and he needed to make sure he did everything he could to secure the safety and future of the one woman he loved more than anything.

◆ ◆ ◆

Aiden woke up with a crick in his neck. Okay, so he'd have to get used to sleeping with Kristen in his arms.

His left arm was completely asleep, so he rolled his wrist and squeezed his hand a few times until he could feel his fingers again. Then he ran his fingers down her soft skin. Even the tingling of his arm coming back didn't detour him from his goal.

When he cupped her perfect breast in his hand, she moved slightly. He moaned softly as he bent his head down and licked his way around her perfect nipples. She moved just a little more.

He looked up at her as he sucked a nipple into his mouth and nibbled on it lightly.

He watched her green eyes open slowly and smiled.

"You're very hard to wake," he said against her skin.

"Who said I was asleep?" She joked and pushed her hands into his hair.

He chuckled and continued his path down her perfect skin. He loved that they slept in the nude. He tugged her new cream sheets away from her long legs and ran his hands over them.

"Sexy, silky legs." He glanced up at her, then heard her sigh with pleasure.

"Hmm?" she said, looking down at him.

"Your legs stop my heart. The first day I saw you, the wind had caught your skirt and . . ." He whistled softly. "Best pair of legs I've ever seen."

"For me, it was that smile of yours." She looked at him like she was seeing him for the first time and her smile dissipated a little. "It's crooked."

He teased, "So, I point out your perfections and you point out my flaws."

"No, your smile is perfect." Her smile was back and she ran her hands through his hair. "Perfectly rugged and sexy as hell." She pulled him closer. He was lost in her eyes as she tugged him back up to her mouth.

When he sank into her slowly, he felt like his heart was exploding. Their rhythm grew faster, and his body began to shake as he held himself back, waiting for her to finish first.

Her legs were wrapped around his hips, driving him faster. As her arms went around his stomach, he knew he couldn't hold back much longer. She held on to him tightly. Her chest pushed up against his, her breath falling over his heated skin.

When he finally felt her convulse around him, he took a chance and leaned closer to her ear.

"I love you," he said against her skin as he felt himself empty completely.

◆　◆　◆

"Did you mean what you said?" she asked a few minutes later. His body had cooled and he knew he was probably crushing her underneath him. He rolled a little until she snuggled next to him, her face resting on his chest. She let out a deep sigh and propped her chin on her hands.

He smiled down at her. "Every word."

"But . . . so soon?" Her eyes moved over his chest.

"When you know it's right . . ." He shrugged.

"I've never said those words to a man before."

He put a finger over her lips. "Don't say them until you're sure."

She nodded and then smiled.

"I was so afraid today." He ran his hands through her hair and noticed her frown.

"You were?" She closed her eyes on a sigh. "It's seriously going to be hard to step foot in another elevator."

He pulled her chin up until she opened her eyes. "I'll be there with you until you feel safe again."

She changed the subject. "You made quite the impression on Amy."

"She's something." He chuckled softly. "She reminds me of my sister, Ashley."

"Oh?" She shifted a little on his chest.

"Not just in looks, but in spunk."

Kristen laughed. "She was always the one getting us in trouble. I may have a wilder sense of style, but she's got the crazy personality."

He played with the tips of her hair. "Ashley is the same way."

"I remember, there was this terrible boy. Logan something . . ." Kristen said with a frown. "Anyway, he tortured us all the way through school. I think he started on Amy in kindergarten. Well, around junior high school, she'd had enough, so she came up with a plan to get back at him by putting itching powder in his gym shoes. We spent almost two weeks planning it out, and when we finally had enough guts to sneak into the boys' locker room, we accidentally got the coaches' cleats instead." Aiden laughed. "Mr. Kentson couldn't walk for almost a week. Of course, no one knew who had done it, and we never told a soul."

He pulled her closer. "Did you ever get back at the boy?"

"No. He moved away shortly after that. To this day, Amy can't stand boys with blue eyes. Maybe that's why she likes you." She snuggled closer and yawned as she rested her head against his chest.

♦ ♦ ♦

Kristen woke the next morning sore. When she tried to move, her knees and elbows screamed at her.

"Here," Aiden said, just above her. She looked up and was thankful he held a glass of water and some aspirin.

"Thanks." She scooted up and leaned against her new headboard to swallow the pills.

"I have an ice pack." He held up a plastic bag filled with ice. He wrapped it in a washcloth and pulled the sheets away from her. For a moment, she was embarrassed about her nudity, but when he focused on getting the ice on her knees, she relaxed a little.

Then she noticed his frown as he looked her bruised body over. When she focused on it, she sighed. "I've had worse." She looked up into his eyes. "Trust me. When I bruise, it's bad for the first two days, and then it all goes away quickly."

"My mother is the same way. The rest of us in my family . . ." He smiled up at her. "It takes a lot to bruise us."

She watched as he tucked the blankets back around her. She really was enjoying finally having a bed again. Her back wasn't hurting her as much and she actually slept all night long again. Not to mention that it was wonderful to sit on a sofa, and such a nice one at that.

"I've made some breakfast." He stood up and looked down at her. "You stay put. I'll bring it in to you."

"Wow, breakfast in bed." She hummed. "A girl could get spoiled like this," she called after him as he walked out of the room.

She leaned back and threw her hands over her head and stretched. Her arms ached a little, and her back was begging for a hot shower, but all in all, she was alive and wasn't going to complain.

He carried in two plates piled with pancakes and eggs, then sat next to her. After getting more comfortable, he handed her a plate. "You could use a TV in here." He nodded to the empty spot on her dresser.

"I used to have one in here," she said after taking a bite of her eggs. "These are delicious." She shoveled more onto her fork.

"Thanks." He beamed and took a big bite of his own.

"You know, most men don't bother with learning how to cook."

"I had a crash course. One summer, my sisters got tired of mac and cheese and grilled cheese sandwiches."

"The first few months I lived on my own, I lived on that stuff, plus ramen noodles."

"Another great staple." He turned a little. "Why don't we go look at televisions before heading to my folks later?"

"I've already put a big dent in my insurance money." She sighed and dreamed about watching TV in bed, curled up next to him.

"I'm buying." He smiled. "Besides, I need a new Blu-ray player. Mine's on the fritz."

"I can't let you buy me a TV." She set her almost-empty plate on her new nightstand and moved to get up.

"You won't be letting me. I want to." He stood and picked up her discarded plate and the ice pack she'd set down, which was now just a bunch of water. Her knees were a little stiff, but they felt better than before. "Go, shower. We can at least go and look." He walked out of the room quickly, not giving her a chance to respond as he cleaned up after her.

She almost crossed her arms over her chest and stomped her foot behind his back, but figured since she was still standing there nude, it wouldn't have the same effect. When had she lost control? When had he started bossing her around?

Did he really think she would let him buy her a TV? Did he think she couldn't take care of herself?

She started to go into the bathroom, but then turned back around and quickly made the bed.

She was halfway through her shower when the glass doors slid open and a very naked Aiden stepped in. Instantly, his hands were on her hips as he stepped under the spray.

"It's not a big enough shower to share," she said, holding on to him so she wouldn't lose her balance.

"I know, but I think we can make do." He pulled her closer and ran his mouth over her neck.

She felt goose bumps rise all over her body and her knees started to go weak. When he kissed her again, her body instantly responded, and she realized she'd lost control in that area of her life as well.

By the time they had finished the shower, her entire body was relaxed. Even her knees felt better. She dressed in a spring skirt and blouse, since she'd peeked at the weather app on her phone and had seen that it was supposed to be in the midseventies for the day.

She loved Colorado. Spring and fall were her favorite seasons. She loved it when the leaves turned to bright orange and yellows and the cooler weather rushed down from the foothills.

But spring had to be her all-time favorite season. Though another spring snowstorm could still sweep in from the north, the flowers had begun to bloom, and just the smell of the grass turning green or the leaves starting to pop out made her smile. If she was lucky, she'd get a chance to see the cherry blossoms in the park before they all floated away.

They spent a few hours going from one electronics store to the next. She drooled over the new smart TVs and desperately wished it was in her budget to get one for her room.

After the theft, her folks had given her their old flat-screen TV and DVD player, which currently sat in her living room. She'd had two nice flat screens before, which Rod had taken and she missed dearly. But she hadn't looked at getting new ones since. She loved that they had so many apps on them, including the ability to Skype.

As much as she wanted a new, high-tech TV, she was thankful when they left the second store empty-handed. There was no way she was going to let Aiden buy her a television. It went against everything she had been raised to believe.

Even though he'd said those three words to her, she still felt their relationship was too new for big gifts like that. She'd never heard those three words said to her, outside of her parents and Amy. She didn't know what to think about a man saying *I love you* to her. Especially after her track record. Could she afford to put herself in a position where she felt completely exposed? Did she have enough trust in him? More importantly, in herself?

"See anything you like?" he asked, causing her eyes to roam over his shoulders. Oh yeah, she saw something she liked very much.

They were at their third store and she'd found yet another great TV. This one was curved and could also do 3-D. She had on the funky little glasses and was enjoying a Disney movie.

"This is so cool." She smiled up at him and held out the other pair of glasses for him to try. He slid them on and she admired just how sexy he looked in glasses. His dark eyebrows rose a little as he looked at the screen.

When he smiled, she felt her knees turn weak, so she reached out and took his arm to steady herself.

"Are your knees hurting?" He took hold of her. "I shouldn't have pushed you so much today."

"No, it's you. You do this to me." She reached up to play with the edge of the glasses. "You make my knees turn to jelly."

His frown slowly turned up. "You're going to say something like that to me in here?" He pulled her close and she felt what he meant as the bulge in his jeans grew.

"Sorry, it's the glasses. You're like a very sexy Clark Kent." She ran a finger over his chin and loved the stubble that was there. "Come on, let's get out of here." He started to remove the glasses, but she stopped him.

"Let me just take a picture." She held up her phone and he laughed.

"Only if you're included," he said in a low tone.

She looked at him and frowned.

"What? You have this sexy-librarian look going on." He pulled her closer. "You have your fantasies, I have mine."

CHAPTER
SEVENTEEN

Two hours later, they walked into his parents' place and were instantly bombarded with questions from his sisters. He really did love them, but sometimes they just didn't know when to shut up.

By the time everyone had finally sat around the table, they had asked Kristen every question under the sun. Of course, she'd smiled and laughed as she answered each and every one of them. She'd been lucky enough to get in a few questions of her own.

Even his mom and stepdad had sat back and listened as the girls chatted on. But what had absolutely topped it all off was when Kristen had asked Amber what was up between her and Tom.

Amber had actually started choking on air and had turned a little red in the face. When she'd recovered, she shrugged and quickly changed the subject as she kept sending glances at Aiden.

He didn't mind that his sister was dating, he even encouraged it, but not with his friends from school. Especially those whom he knew exactly what was on their minds.

Not that Tom was a bad guy. But he was so much older than his little sister.

"Kristen, you and my brother will have to come and see me downtown next month. I've made one of the leads in *Wicked*. I play Glinda." She beamed.

She'd found out last month and had been working overtime with practices and fittings. Aiden loved that his sister was an arts major at Denver University and that she'd been hired on by the Buell Theatre downtown.

She'd been in several plays and had been magnificent in each one. He didn't know where she got her talent and voice, but he doubted it was from their mother's side.

Kristen glanced at him before diverting her eyes back to Amber. "You're in a play?" She leaned forward. "I've always wanted to go to one. How exciting. Congratulations."

Amber gushed for the rest of the dinner, and the conversation turned toward his sisters instead of his relationship with Kristen.

By the time they walked out of his parents' house, he could tell Kristen was tired. She held on to him as she walked down the sidewalk toward his car.

"Knees hurting?" He wrapped his arm around her.

She nodded. "I should have brought some more aspirin."

"I'm sure my mother has some." He started to walk back to see.

She shook her head and tugged him toward his car. "I'll be all right. Really." She smiled up at him. He would have done anything to make her more comfortable.

They walked the rest of the way to his car. When he got in, he turned to her. "Your place or mine?"

She leaned back. "I'm thinking of a hot bath and bed."

"I'll take you home. Will you still feel up to brunch with your folks tomorrow?"

"It's not that easy getting out of a meal with my parents. They don't take no for an answer."

"Think you'll be okay?" he asked.

She sighed and closed her eyes as she rested back. "I just need a hot bath and sleep."

"Speaking of plans, I have this thing next weekend." He glanced at her. "It's just a charity dinner and I was hoping you'd come along with me."

She leaned forward. "Charity?"

He shrugged. "I worked on a project downtown for a women's shelter, and to thank everyone, they're having a big get-together."

She was silent for a while. "Is it formal?"

He peeked at her. "Sort of, why?"

"Because I haven't had a chance to fully replace my wardrobe yet."

"What you're wearing will be fine." He reached over and took her hand.

"Right." She chuckled. "I'd love to go. Was it a project for R&S? I don't remember hearing anything about a women's shelter in the last staff meeting."

"No, it's something I was working on on the side," he said. It was the truth; the project hadn't even been on UD's books. He'd donated his time to help out after he'd heard about the project from his mother, whose close friend ran the place.

"I've always wanted to do charity work." She leaned back again. "But, as it is, I don't have enough time to finish my own projects." She rested her eyes and they drove in silence the rest of the way to her apartment.

He had to shake her gently to wake her up when they arrived. After walking her up to her door and kissing her good night, he drove back to his condo.

When he walked in, he realized just how empty the place felt. As he crawled into bed, he missed the warmth of Kristen next to him and just couldn't get comfortable without her pressed up against his body.

The next morning, he woke up sore and grouchy and he was sure of one thing—there was no way he wanted to spend another night without Kristen in his arms.

He was also thinking it was time he talked to her about his intentions with R&S. But first, he wanted to discuss it with Steven and Paul. He didn't want to jeopardize either relationship at this point.

♦ ♦ ♦

Kristen was soaking in her hot bath when her phone buzzed next to her. Glancing at the number, she smiled.

"So?" Amy's voice sounded a little breathless.

"All I can say is, I love his family."

"Did they give you the third degree?"

She laughed. "His sisters did, until I mentioned Tom to Amber. I think there's something there that she doesn't want her big brother to know about."

"Oh, sista's got a secret."

"Are you in the bath? Is Aiden there?" She chuckled when Amy made a sexy growl sound.

"Yes and no. I'm alone, soaking away my sore muscles from yesterday."

"From the elevator? You said you didn't get hurt." She heard worry in her friend's voice.

"I didn't. Well, bruised a little. My knees took the brunt of the destruction." She glanced down at her swollen kneecaps. Her arms and hands didn't hurt at all, just her legs. She flexed her toes. "What are you doing?"

"I'd like to tell you I have a tall, dark, sexy man wrapped around me, but the truth is I'm watching TV. Isn't it a sad state when two hot women like us are spending our Saturday nights home alone?"

"I'm choosing to be alone tonight." She leaned back, sinking farther into the hot water, letting the bubbles cover the bruises.

"Sure, rub it in. Hey!" She heard Amy gasp. "Hang on a sec." She heard the phone muffle as Amy moved around. "Oh my God!"

"What?" Kristen sat up in the water, instantly concerned. "Are you okay?" Amy didn't respond at first. Not until Kristen repeated her name almost half a dozen times.

"Are you sitting down?" Amy asked.

"Duh! I'm in the tub," she repeated.

"You'd better get out. I don't want you accidentally drowning."

"What is it?" she growled out.

"Well, I had the TV on mute on a local news station. They were doing this report about an event that's going to take place next weekend. Then your guy's picture flashed on the screen."

Kristen smiled, remembering Aiden asking her to the event. She leaned back and closed her eyes. "Yeah, Aiden invited me to the event. It's for some women's shelter downtown."

"Well, that's not the part you need to hold on to your socks about."

"Okay?" She sat up.

"When I finally found my remote and un-muted, they were saying Aiden Scott was owner of Urban Development, one of the most successful development firms in Denver." There was a pause. "I thought you said he worked at R&S?"

Everyone who was anyone in development and architecture in Colorado knew about Urban Development. R&S had even worked with them over the last few years on several high-profile projects.

"That can't be right."

"Hang on." Amy could hear clicking through the phone. "Um, no, it's correct. I'm on their Web site and it says the CEO is Aiden Scott. There's even a damn sexy picture of him."

"What's he doing at R&S, then?" Her heart sank.

"I don't know. Maybe he's priming to take over, or worse, take them down."

Pain shot through Amy's chest. "He's going to take over Row and Stein," she said, under her breath. "I saw him in a meeting with the shareholders the other day. I thought it was weird when I didn't see Steven or Paul there." She felt like a complete idiot.

"Wait, you don't know that. Maybe there's something more to the story."

"No, it makes sense. Do they know he's there just to push them out? They built this company from scratch. My father has told me horror stories of how Steven struggled for the first few years until he brought Paul in. He can't do this to them." She jumped from the tub, almost slipping and falling. "I have to call my parents."

"Krissy, don't jump to conclusions."

"He lied to me." She wrapped a towel around herself, feeling her anger heat every inch of her body.

"We don't know what his intentions are yet."

"No, but we know what they aren't. He's not just another designer. He came into R&S, into my house, my family, my friends, determined to take them down."

"Kris—"

"I can't talk now." She quickly hung up and punched her father's number.

Half an hour later, she was no closer to understanding Aiden's game than when she had started. Her father didn't know anything about it and didn't think it was his place to call Steven Row to find out. He'd suggested that she ask them herself next week at work.

When she finally crawled into bed, her entire body pulsed with sadness, spreading out from her heart.

She had horrible dreams about Aiden in which Steven's and Paul's heads were on small little flies. The office was transformed into tiny cutouts and stuck on a huge spider's web with the title "Urban Development" etched in odd-looking letters above, much like the lettering in *Charlotte's Web*. Steven and Paul struggled to get free from the web as a very large, dark spider with Aiden's head crawled toward them.

When he got closer, he opened his mouth and fangs hung out of his blood-soaked lips.

She woke with a jolt and glanced at her alarm clock. It was a quarter past three and she knew without a doubt that she wasn't going to get any more sleep that night.

When Aiden called her later that morning to see if she was feeling better, she made an excuse that she wasn't and canceled the lunch with her folks. He'd tried to convince her to let him come over, but she'd shut him down quickly.

She couldn't deal with seeing him yet. Not until she knew exactly what he was doing at R&S. Not until she could control her hurt and anger over his personal betrayal. He'd lied to her. And she'd fallen for yet another man who could manipulate her feelings. She was almost as angry with herself as she was with him.

She spent half of the day in bed, the other half watching television as she lay on her new sofa. She had iced her knees, and by evening, the swelling was almost gone.

Amy had stopped by quickly around lunch and they had devised a plan of action. She wasn't going to walk into the office tomorrow unprepared. She was never going to be unprepared again when it came to men.

CHAPTER
EIGHTEEN

Aiden was running late. He'd hoped to meet Kristen out front and ride up the elevator with her. When he texted her that he was outside, she had replied that she was already at her desk and had taken the stairs.

He walked into the office only five minutes late, but he had to immediately go into a meeting with the board. He'd come to a decision early last week and his lawyers were drawing up all the paperwork. The board just had a few other items they needed to discuss with him.

After clearing it with Steven and Paul, he was relieved to finally be able to tell her everything he'd been keeping from her.

He had planned to see her after the meeting, but when he walked by her desk, it was empty. He asked Carla where she was and she told him that she was out at a job site and wouldn't be back in the office until tomorrow.

He'd texted her but hadn't received a message back. When he tried to call her after five, it went directly to her voice mail.

He knew he only had until the end of the week at R&S and really needed to talk to her before returning to work at his own offices. He had planned on telling her everything over dinner this week, but by

Thursday evening, he still hadn't had a chance to see her, let alone talk to her. He knew she was busy at work, since he'd been running around the office himself.

When he walked into the offices Friday morning—his last official day at R&S—and found out that she was again out on a job, his frustration level blew. He couldn't figure out why she had been avoiding his calls, his voice mails, and his text messages. But he was determined to end all the running around that very moment.

"Aiden?" Steven stopped him from walking out of the doors. "Got a sec?" He nodded toward his office.

"Sure." He followed the man.

"Morning, Aiden," Paul said, standing up to shake his hand.

"Paul." He shook the man's hand.

"We know you're probably going to head out soon, but we just wanted to thank you again for everything that you're doing," Steven said, walking around his desk and sitting down.

He smiled. "I'm just happy we could make everything work out. I hear you're moving to Florida."

"Got a little place lined up along the Emerald Coast. The missus and I will be moving before the first snowfall," Steven said.

"I'm sure my folks will be visiting you guys. They love it down there."

"I know. They're the ones that turned us on to the place."

"We have something for you," Paul said, pulling out a box wrapped in silver paper and a black bow. "To thank you for everything." He handed it to Aiden.

"You didn't have to do that. I mean, I am getting a very successful business in return."

They laughed. "We know you could have come in and cleared the place out, but with the negotiations going the way they have . . ." Steven shrugged. "I'm sure when we tell the staff today at the meeting, everyone is going to be thrilled."

He felt his stomach drop. With all the running around this week, trying to get some time alone with Kristen, he'd forgotten about the staff meeting. He glanced down at his watch and frowned. The meeting was set to start in half an hour.

"Well?" Steven nudged him. "Aren't you going to open it?"

He looked down and quickly tore open the package. It was a black leather box, and when he opened it, there was a shiny new set of silver drafting tools engraved with his name.

"Thank you." He looked up and smiled. "It's perfect."

"You know where to find us if you need anything," Paul said, standing back.

He excused himself and walked back to his office and dialed Kristen's cell phone. He usually didn't make personal calls from the office, but since she was avoiding his calls, he knew she would answer one coming from work.

"Hello?" she answered on the second ring.

"Are you avoiding me?" he asked, holding his breath.

He heard a silence, then listened as she made an excuse and stepped away from someone she'd been talking to.

"No." He could hear the lie in her tone.

"Why?" he asked.

"I'm at a job site."

"I know, we're supposed to have a staff meeting in half an hour."

"Yes, I know. I'll be there."

"You haven't answered my question." He was beginning to worry that he'd moved too fast, or not fast enough.

"Let's not do this over the phone. I'll be back in the office in ten minutes."

He glanced at his watch. "Where are you?"

"The place on Market Street. I'm leaving now."

"I'll meet you halfway."

"No . . ." she started to say, but then was quiet. "Okay. There's a coffee shop at the corner of Sixteenth and Lawrence."

"I know it. I'll be there." He hung up and tried to figure out his next move as he walked out of the building.

The whole week he'd been playing over his family dinner. Had his sisters said or done something to upset her? He couldn't remember anything.

He'd toiled over it all week, and since she'd been playing cat and mouse with him, he hadn't had a chance to ask her directly.

He'd even thought about showing up at her place and banging on the door. But something had told him that wouldn't have gone over well. He'd even wished he'd had Amy's number so he could ask her.

Less than five minutes later, he walked into the coffee shop and saw Kristen standing in line. He walked up behind her and wrapped his arm around her waist. He hadn't realized how much he'd missed her until he felt her in his arms again.

"Hey." He smiled down at her and felt her stiffen a little in his arms. She quickly recovered.

"Do you want anything?" She pointed to the menu since they were next in line.

"Besides you?" He shook his head. "I'd like an explanation of why you've been avoiding me."

"Coffee first. I didn't get a chance to get some before my meeting."

He stayed close to her as she placed her order. They waited for her name to be called and then walked over and sat in a booth near the back wall.

She took a sip and closed her eyes. She looked a little weary, but he figured it was due to the early morning meeting.

"Rough time?"

Her eyes opened and she zeroed in on his. "Are you taking over Row and Stein?" she said in one quick breath.

He felt his heart kick and his palms go damp. When he nodded, he could see the anger flood into her green eyes.

"There's nothing more I want to say to you. The moment you sign the papers, you'll have my resignation on your desk." She started to get up, but he trapped her there with his hand.

"Kristen, this isn't some hostile takeover," he pleaded with her.

"I don't care what you think it is." She jerked her hand back. "You lied to me." She started to gather up her bags.

"I never lied to you." He stood up and reached for her, telling himself that what he had done was only withhold vital information from her.

"You didn't tell me everything. That's the same as lying." She shoved her bag over her shoulder and moved past him, leaving her almost-full coffee on the table.

"Wait a minute." He followed her. "What's this all about?" He took her arm as she exited the building. He felt his heart kick at the thought of losing her.

She jerked her arm away from him. "This is about friendship, and you've made it very clear that all it means to you is dollar signs." She turned toward him. "Or did you think I wouldn't find out who you really are? Urban Development."

"I never hid who I was." He crossed his arms over his chest, not understanding why it mattered.

"You didn't come right out and tell everyone," she hissed in a low tone.

"No." He took a deep breath. "I didn't."

Her eyes narrowed. "I believed you when you said Steven was a friend of your family."

"He is." He tilted his head, wanting her to believe him.

"How could you do this to him?" she whispered.

He felt his palms go sweaty and reached for her once more. He didn't think he would have time now to explain it to her, but if it meant keeping her, he would do everything in his power to hold on to their relationship. Even if it meant cutting his losses with the deal. "You don't have all the facts, I'm not—"

"I don't need facts," she interrupted. "I've heard all about the last time Urban Development took over a business."

He cringed. "This is different."

"Is it?" She started walking toward their building again.

He took her arm and spun her around. "Yes, it is. This is personal."

She glared at him and then looked down at his hand, which was holding her arm. "Let go of me," she said under her breath.

"I can't," he whispered.

♦ ♦ ♦

Kristen was running on pure adrenaline. She'd missed breakfast and had only had a few sips of her coffee. She groaned when she realized she'd left it back in the coffee shop, then glanced back and saw Aiden rushing to follow her.

She'd desperately needed the kick of caffeine before what she could only imagine would be a very uncomfortable meeting.

"Let me walk with you. Everything will be explained at the meeting." He jogged to keep up with her.

She jerked her arm away again. "Don't you get it? It doesn't matter what happens in the meeting. You betrayed my trust."

He took a step back like she'd slapped him.

"Kristen."

She shook her head and fought back the tears. She'd cried too much this last week and didn't want to give him any more.

"We'd better go or we'll be late for your big meeting." She turned and started walking and felt him following her.

When she walked into the building, she headed toward the stairs. But he took hold of her arm and started walking toward the elevators.

"Aiden," she said in a low voice. She felt her breath speed up and her heart rate skyrocket the closer they got to the metal doors.

"Don't fight it." He ran his hand down her back, sending shivers up her spine. Why did her body still react this way to him even though her heart hurt so much?

"Don't . . ." She tried to pull her arm free. "I can't . . ." She started to feel light-headed.

"At least let me do this for you," he said next to her ear as the metal doors slid open slowly.

All week long, she'd avoided elevators at all cost. The one she'd been trapped in had been closed down for three days, and now it was back up and running. This time, however, they stepped into a different car and she felt her knees go completely weak.

His arm was around her as he hit the button to their floor. When the doors slid closed, he nudged her until her back was up against the mirrored wall.

"Look at me." His voice broke through the cloud of fear. Then she focused only on his dark eyes. "Good." He smiled and she felt the rest of her body melt at the sexy curve of his lips. "Forget everything." He took a step closer to her, and time seemed to stop completely. Even the need for breathing halted.

His hand came up and he brushed the back of his fingers down her cheek. "I don't care what happens now. Just know that I love you," he said before his lips found hers.

She couldn't stop herself from responding to his kiss as his mouth tilted over hers. His hands were feather light as they ran up and down her back, her arms, pulling her, holding her closer. She felt his pulse jump against her hands that lay on his chest.

She'd been a fool to try and deny the fact that she'd fallen for him. Completely.

When the car slowed down, he pulled back. "Think of this, of me, every time you step into one of these again." He smiled down at her and ran his hand over her wet cheek. "I'm sorry if I hurt you. I hope you'll give me a chance to explain my actions."

She hadn't realized she'd been crying until that moment. All her fears and emotions seemed to spring forward at once. Just the thought that Aiden had betrayed her, her friends, had her eyes burning. Using the back of her hand, she wiped her face dry as they stepped out onto their floor.

"Take a moment." He nodded to the restroom. "I'll see you in the meeting." He turned and walked into the front doors at R&S.

She rushed to the restroom, afraid of what she looked like. Expecting to be pale and frazzled, she went to the mirror and was shocked. Her cheeks were pink, her lips red from his kisses, and her eyes . . . her eyes were completely dreamy looking. Like she'd just been kissed by the man she loved.

She closed her eyes and leaned on the sink and took a couple cleansing breaths.

She washed her face, put on some fresh lip gloss, and straightened her shoulders. She was completely prepared for the meeting.

When she walked into the crowded conference room, Aiden, Steven, and Paul were all standing at the front of the room. Aiden watched her walk in and she couldn't control her heart from fluttering when she noticed the way he looked at her.

Damn him for playing her. She raised her chin up and met his eyes. She'd typed up her resignation last night, just in case he wanted to go through with his plan of tearing up her friends' company. It felt wonderful to know that she wouldn't be his employee and fall into his trap. He may have played her, but that didn't mean he would win the prize.

CHAPTER NINETEEN

Aiden stood next to Steven and Paul and listened as they explained what was in store for the company in the next few months. They told everyone how Aiden had bought them out and that the business was being merged with Urban Development.

He watched the faces in the room and knew that people were scared of some of the changes. Everyone except Kristen, who still looked furious at him. She refused to make eye contact across the crowded room. He knew he could convince her to give him a second chance, since he'd seen the heat in her eyes after they'd stepped out of the elevators. He'd felt the passion in her lips as he'd kissed her.

He wished more than anything that he could have brought her into the fold. He felt terrible when he looked at her and she wouldn't return his gaze. He never meant to hide anything from her. Seeing the tears in her eyes had broken his heart, but he knew that once he had a chance to explain, everything would be smoothed out. At least he prayed it would be.

When Steven nudged him in the ribs, he realized he'd been called to speak.

"Hi." He cleared his throat and pulled his eyes away from Kristen and focused on his speech. "Most of you know me already. I want to assure everyone that not much is going to change."

"Is it true we're moving?" someone called out from the crowd.

"Yes, in the next few months, we will be migrating everyone to our new offices five blocks away. There's plenty of room. Plus, no more paying for parking in the garage since there's free parking at the new location."

"Whoop!" someone shouted.

Aiden smiled. "Now, there will be some minor changes." He glanced around the room and spotted the three employees that would not be making the move. It was inevitable that he'd have to let go of a few staff members. He sighed and then looked back at Kristen. "We hope that everyone will feel very welcome at UD and that this can be the start of something great."

Everyone clapped as he stepped back. For the next few minutes, he stood by and shook everybody's hands as they exited the conference room. Steven, Paul, and he answered a bunch of other questions and he was thankful when he noticed Kristen standing at the back of the line.

When she finally approached Steven, he could see tears in her eyes.

"Why?" she said as Steven took her hand in his. "Why didn't you tell me you wanted to retire?"

The older man pulled her closer and hugged her. "I know you too well. You would have tried to talk us out of it. Besides, when I ran the idea by your father, he's the one that suggested I keep it from you."

He watched her eyes heat. "He did what?"

Steven chuckled. "Oh no, now I've gotten him in trouble, haven't I?"

"Don't worry about it. I'm sure he has an explanation." She glanced over at Paul. "Will you be heading south too?"

"Nope, Belinda and I are heading farther into the mountains. We've decided to make our Winter Park place our permanent residence."

She smiled. "Well, I know you'll enjoy retirement." Then she looked back over at Steven and shook her head. "You, on the other hand, will be bored by the end of the first week."

They all laughed. Then her eyes zeroed in on Aiden. "Mr. Scott." She turned and walked out of the room without another word.

"You stepped in it this time, son." Steven slapped his back.

He nodded and watched her disappear around the corner, toward her desk.

"I should have told her sooner." He felt his head actually spinning. Funny, he'd heard people use the expression, but until that very moment, he had never experienced it before.

"He's got it bad," Paul said beside him. "But, Aiden, we're grateful you kept your word."

"Can you blame him? Krissy is a good kid. Fine looking too. She's made of strong stuff. You don't stumble upon a woman like that very often." Aiden was slapped again on the back but wasn't sure who had done it this time since his eyes were still on the corner where Kristen had disappeared.

"When you do, you do whatever it takes to hold on to 'em."

The two men shook their heads as they walked out of the conference room. They were right. Of course, he knew they were.

The way she'd responded to him in the elevator told him that he still had a chance. All he needed to do was step up his game. And he knew just the next step to take.

After pulling out his cell phone from his pocket, he called the one person who could help him win Krissy back.

◆　◆　◆

Kristen spent Friday night with Amy at her place. They did each other's nails and drank two bottles of their favorite wine. By the time she crashed in Amy's spare bedroom, she had convinced herself that she was better off without men. Any man. All men. Especially men who were tall and had dark hair, sexy chocolate eyes, and an unforgettably dashing crooked smile.

By the time Amy dropped Kristen back off at her apartment, she was once again questioning her own motives. Listening to Steven and Paul talk yesterday in the meeting really made it sound like it had been all their idea.

She knew in her heart that she wasn't mad at Aiden for helping out a friend of the family. But she just couldn't get over the fact that he'd kept his true mission hidden from her.

For some reason, the betrayal had stung more than when Rod had stolen all of her stuff. Maybe it was because she had fallen for Aiden completely.

She thought about it as she climbed the stairs to her apartment. When she reached the second floor landing, she was surprised to see Amber leaning against her door.

"There you are!" Amber rushed over to her.

"What? Is something wrong?" Instantly she was on guard.

"Uh?" Amber blinked at her a few times. "Oh, no, nothing that you can't fix." She tugged on her arm until Kristen opened the door. Then she reached down and picked up a large black bag that was sitting at the foot of her door.

"I need your help." Amber walked into Kristen's apartment and looked around. "Nice place." She turned back toward her.

"Thanks." Kristen frowned. "What's all this about?" She set her purse down.

"Like I said . . ." Amber placed her arms on her hips. "I need your help." She walked over and sat down on the edge of her sofa. "Since you pretty much canceled on my brother for tonight's big party"— Amber looked up at her with her soft blue eyes—"he convinced me to tag along with him."

Kristen's heart sank a little more. She'd been looking forward to going to the event. She now understood that Steven and Paul had actually wanted Aiden to take over . . . and that Aiden had been told specifically by her two friends not to tell her about the merger. Everything had changed. She really felt like she owed Aiden the chance to explain his actions. As Kristen came out of her thoughts she realized Amber was still talking to her.

"But I couldn't tell him that I already had plans with a certain man whose name I can't mention at the moment." She winked at her and Kristen knew she was talking about Tom. "Anyway, I figured since you got me into this mess, you simply had to get me out of it."

"What are you talking about?"

Amber smiled, then reached down and pulled out an armful of emerald-green silk. When she held it up, Kristen realized it was a very sleek evening gown.

"You had that wadded up in that bag?"

Amber giggled. "It's supposed to look wrinkled. See." She shook it out and sure enough, the material looked gorgeous crushed. "It goes perfectly with your eyes." She walked toward her, holding it up.

"Oh no!" She held her hands up as she backed up a few steps. "I'm not going any—"

"You simply have to. I can't cancel on T—on my date." Amber blushed. "And I can't tell Aiden why I won't be showing up at the party."

"I'm not going. Besides, I said some pretty mean stuff to your brother yesterday. I'm sure he doesn't—" Kristen felt her heart fall. She hadn't realized how deeply she felt about him, until now.

"If he could forgive Ash and me for replacing his deodorant with Icy Hot when we were kids, then I'm sure he can forgive you. Besides, everyone in the family knows how crazy he is about you and how crazy you are about him." She smiled and held up the dress in front of her.

It was perfect. The long flowing material hung around her ankles. There was a sexy slit up one side that would go to just above her knees. The shoulder straps were thin and went down the back in a sexy V.

"I have something else . . ." Amber pushed the dress into Kristen's hands then rushed back to her bag and pulled out a pair of cream-colored heels.

Kristen shook her head. "I . . . I can't . . ."

"Sure you can. You're really saving my butt here. Come on . . ." She started tugging on her hand. "I'll help you get ready. The party starts in less than an hour."

◆　◆　◆

Forty minutes later, Kristen stood in front of her mirror and blinked a few times. Amber knew more about hair and makeup than Amy and she combined. For that matter, more than anyone she'd ever met before.

Her long hair was piled up on top of her head and long ringlets fell around her face. Her makeup, well, she'd never seen herself look so good before. She felt like Cinderella after her fairy godmother had come to her rescue.

"Perfect." Amber stood back. "Too bad you don't have some pearls."

Kristen shook her head. "Everything I had was stolen."

"Aiden told me about that." She glanced down at her watch. "Oh my, you're going to be late." She turned Kristen around and hugged her. "I've arranged for a car to pick you up. It should be here by now." She rushed to the window in the living room. Kristen followed her.

"It's down there. Thank you so much for doing this." She hugged her again.

Kristen laughed. "I don't know how you talked me into it."

"Now you know how Aiden felt growing up. Except there were two of us convincing him."

Kristen started walking toward the door.

"Oh wait." Amber rushed back to her bag.

"What now? Do you have a mouse that's going to turn into a footman in that thing?"

"No, but I do have a clutch that goes with the dress." She handed her a small green purse.

"You think of everything."

"Not everything. If I had, you'd have a string of pearls around your neck and wrist." She smiled and hugged her again. "Have fun. I'll flip the lock when I leave."

Kristen looked at her and then nodded when she decided she really did like the girl.

When she stepped off the last stair, she almost fell face forward when she saw the car that Amber had been talking about. The long black stretch limo was parked right in front of her building.

She started walking toward it, expecting the driver to jump out and open the door for her. She'd never ridden in a limo before, but she'd seen plenty of movies and knew how it all worked.

But instead, the back door flew open, and she watched in shock as a very sexy Aiden stepped out. His black suit fit him perfectly, giving him a James Bond look. His hair was slicked back a little, showing off the angles of his perfect face.

He held a single white rose out to her as his smile grew. Even in the fading light of dusk, she could see the heat in his eyes as he looked her over.

CHAPTER
TWENTY

She was perfection. There was no other way to describe the way Kristen looked as she walked toward him. The setting sun flashed in her hair, causing the highlights to almost sparkle.

The long, slender dress fit her like a glove. Every curve was on display for him.

Her smile faded when she saw him, and then her eyes heated as she actually noticed him.

"Good evening." He held the rose out for her.

"Hi." She frowned. "Your sister"—she looked back up toward the stairs at the same moment his sister snapped a few pictures with her phone—"is going to die," she said between gritted teeth.

"Don't blame her." He took her hand and started leading her to the limo. His sister continued snapping pictures of them even after he shot her a thank-you look behind Kristen's back.

"After all, she's just the puppet. I'm the one that talked her into it."

Kristen turned toward him. "You?" She swayed in his arms. "You arranged all this?"

He nodded. "Where do you think Amber and Ashley learned it

from?" He chuckled and then helped her into the back of the limo. When he walked around, the driver was holding his door open.

After climbing in beside her, he reached over and pulled her closer so they sat in the middle of the large backseat.

"I have something for you." He pulled out a black package from his jacket pocket.

She blinked a few times as he opened the silk box. Her eyes grew big as she saw the perfect row of pearls that lay on the dark background.

"I . . ." She swallowed. "I can't . . ." Her green eyes looked up to his.

He set the box on his lap, then reached down, took the string of pearls, and helped her fasten them around her neck.

"There, now everything is perfect." He leaned down and placed his lips on the nape of her neck and felt her vibrate under his lips.

"Aiden." It came out as a whisper. "I don't know what to say." She turned back to him. Her eyes looked damp.

"Say you'll forgive me." He took her hand. "I should have told you my plans the second our relationship changed. I shouldn't have kept this from you. No matter what."

"I should have known that with my luck . . ."

He stopped her by putting a finger over her lips. "Don't . . . don't blame this on luck."

"No, I've learned to make my own."

"Then your string of bad luck has ended? And you'll forgive me?"

She nodded and he felt his heart leap.

He pulled her closer until she was almost in his lap. "We don't have to show up to this party."

"Oh no. Your sister didn't twist my hair and put all this stuff on my face for nothing. I want to go show it all off."

"At least tell me we can kiss all the way there." He didn't know if he could get enough alone time with her before they showed up and he'd have to share her with everyone else.

She leaned closer to him and placed her lips softly on his.

By the time they finally arrived at the party, he was having a hard time concentrating as he mingled with the crowd.

He'd attended several functions like this before but had never really enjoyed himself. Tonight was no exception.

He watched Kristen laugh at something Betty said to her. His mother's friend Betty Garrison was rounding a hundred years old, but could still move like a fifty-year-old. The woman was half Kristen's size, but she looked just as elegant as Kristen did. Well, maybe not quite as good.

He'd been pulled into a small group of men who were talking about building permits and what the score was for last night's game. He wanted to be beside Kristen instead.

It took him almost ten minutes to finally pull himself away from the group. He looked over and saw Kristen stepping out onto one of the back patios of the old house where the party was being held. Mrs. Garrison was from one of Denver's oldest and most elite families. The large stone house sat on one of the most famous, largest blocks in Cherry Hills.

When he stepped out onto the patio, he saw that she'd walked down the wide stone stairs and was strolling slowly in the moonlight in a small flower garden. There were a few other couples enjoying the night air, but for the most part, the garden was quiet as everyone enjoyed the drinks and music inside.

"Hi." He walked up beside her and linked his arm with hers.

"Hi." She smiled up at him. "I can just imagine what this place looked like a hundred years ago." She glanced around and smiled. "Probably exactly as it does now."

He nodded and felt a knot in his throat when he looked at her.

"I can almost imagine that we're there now." She sighed as he led her to a stone bench and sat next to her. "With this dress, I almost feel like it is nineteen hundred. All I need is a long pair of gloves and a corset."

"I'd rather believe that you're not wearing anything under that dress." His eyes moved over her.

She smiled at him and leaned against his chest. "Your sister was very insistent that I not have any lines show through."

He groaned. "I can't decide if I'm going to kill her . . . or thank her."

Kristen giggled. "That makes two of us. And to think that before you showed up in the limo, I had decided to trust her completely."

"I learned long ago to always keep one eye open when I'm around those two," he teased.

She gasped. "Do you think she lied about . . ." She bit her bottom lip. "Never mind."

"Oh no, you can't get out of something like that. Spill." He took her arms in his hands.

She closed her eyes and rested back against his shoulder. "I'd better not say anything. Not until after I talk to her."

He was about to insist that she tell him what she was talking about when she turned toward him. When he caught sight of the dreamy look in her eyes, he decided to drop the subject.

"Have I told you that you look beautiful tonight?"

She shook her head lightly. "I think we skipped that part." It came out as a whisper.

He wanted to give her more than just words, but with the party roaring just a few yards away from them, words would have to do for now. He turned her toward him a little until he could look down into her eyes.

"Your beauty is beyond words. It takes my breath away." He reached out and ran a finger over her chin. "Your eyes are like emeralds. Your lips like candy." He leaned down and brushed his mouth lightly over hers.

"Aiden," she said against his skin. "I . . . I never thought . . ."

"Neither did I. I never thought I could fall so hopelessly and madly in love with someone. I never dreamed they would be as wonderful as you are." He leaned down and kissed her again, this time allowing enough passion behind his lips that he felt her heartbeat jump.

"What do you say we make our excuses and get out of here?" she said when she finally pulled away.

"I thought you'd never ask." He placed another kiss on her lips quickly and pulled her up off the bench.

They said the fastest good-byes in history and left. He didn't mind what people thought or said about them. He had plans for the night that were more important than other people's opinions.

As the limo drove them to their next destination, he kept her busy in the backseat by kissing her until he felt like they had melted the leather interior.

When the car finally stopped, she glanced out the window and frowned. "Where are we?"

"I have another surprise for you."

She looked over at him just as the driver opened her door. Aiden jumped out first and then helped her out of the back himself.

"If all went well, you'll have a bag with a change of clothes already inside." He nodded to the large log cabin.

"Where are we?" She turned to him.

"Do you like it?" He stood back and motioned for her to get a better look.

"Yes, it's wonderful, but . . ."

"It's all ours for the rest of the weekend." He took her hand and started to pull her up a large circular staircase.

♦　♦　♦

Kristen was in shock. Her feet wouldn't move. She could have sworn she'd heard Aiden say they were going to spend the rest of the weekend in this giant, gorgeous mansion of a log cabin.

From what she could see—and she could see a lot since the place was lit up like a Christmas tree with white lights—the cabin was three stories tall and probably spanned over six thousand square feet.

She hadn't been paying attention to where the driver had been going, but she could tell they were somewhere in the foothills. They walked up a large spiral staircase and stopped in front of two very big front doors.

"How did you—?" she started to ask, but he just shook his head.

"Let's just say that a friend owed me." He leaned down and pulled out a shiny key from under the mat. "Right where I told her to put it."

"Who?" She frowned as he opened the front door.

He glanced at her from over his shoulder. "My sister." He smiled and opened the door wide.

Warm air hit her shoulders and she realized that it was quite chilly out, especially since she hadn't brought a jacket. She stepped inside the brightly lit cabin.

It was beyond anything she'd ever imagined. The entryway was stunning. There was a three-story stone, double-faced fireplace that ran along the entrance wall. She could see through the large firebox into a sunken living room. When he pulled her around the stone wall, the room opened up.

Long hallways ran on either side of the second-floor balconies; from those, doorways led to rooms on both sides. The top floor looked completely open, like it was a loft that ran the entire length of the building. Everything was held up with large, round logs that were stained and shined like new.

Her eyes moved back down to the main floor, which had hardwood floors covered with beautiful area rugs.

The furniture was a little rustic for her taste, but it certainly matched the house. He took her hand and led her into the living room. She could see a large kitchen near the back of the main floor alongside a beautiful dining room that held one of the biggest tables she'd ever seen.

"This is some spread." She turned toward him.

"Yeah, I've always told Tom his family was just showing off when they built the place."

"Tom?" She shook her head and laughed. "How much does that man owe you for going out with your sister?"

He frowned. "They're not going out."

"Oh right." She tried to hold back her laughter. From the look on Aiden's face, she got the impression that Tom wouldn't make it to next year if she continued to talk about it.

"Amber should have stocked the fridge for us." He walked over and pulled open the door. "Yup. Looks like we're all set until Sunday night."

"I can't stay here that long." She followed him into the room.

"Why not?" He turned toward her.

"I don't have . . ." She looked down at the dress. Although it was beyond lovely, there was no way she was going to spend a weekend in the mountains wearing only an evening gown.

"I did mention that Amber packed a bag for you. It's probably upstairs with my own bag." He tugged her hand and she followed him up the large three-story staircase.

She thought that he would stop on the second floor, but he continued to the top level. She gasped at the room as they stopped at the top of the stairs.

Instead of a loft, it was a huge master suite, which had large windows on every side. A huge four-poster log bed sat in the middle of the big space. The stone fireplace already had a small fire burning.

"Amber probably started this for us," he said as he tossed a few more logs on the fire.

"If you want, you can check to see if she packed everything you will need." He nodded toward two double doors.

She opened the doors wide and walked into the biggest bathroom she'd ever seen. There was an enormous jet tub that sat right in front of a huge window. The glass shower was bigger than her entire bathroom.

Then she noticed the black bag she'd borrowed from Aiden during their trip to Vail and peeked inside. She had to admit, Amber was very thorough.

"Do you have everything?" he asked from the doorway. When she turned and looked at him, he was leaning against the doorjamb. He'd removed his jacket and had rolled up the sleeves of his shirt. James Bond had nothing on him.

She slowly walked to him. "Have I told you how handsome you look tonight?" She ran her fingers down the buttons of his shirt and watched him swallow and shake his head no. "Better than James Bond."

"Which one?" he joked.

"All of them rolled together," she purred next to his lips. "Take me to bed, Mr. Scott." She laughed when he swung her up in his arms and walked across the room to the large bed.

CHAPTER
TWENTY-ONE

It was the hardest thing he'd ever had to do, waiting all night at the charity gala until he could finally have her back in his arms. Even though it had only been a week since he'd held her there, it had felt like a lifetime.

As he peeled off the sexy, tight dress she wore, his hands shook and desire raged inside him. Something deep and primitive called him to take what he wanted, hard and fast. Yet another part of him urged him to go slow and show her romance instead.

When her teeth scraped up his neck, he almost lost his control.

"Why are you fighting it?" she moaned as her hands pushed his shirt off his shoulders.

He tried to clear his thoughts, to go slow so she would enjoy it more. But then her nails raked over his skin and he lost the last strings of his control.

She laughed as he quickly flipped her over onto her stomach. His hands spread her thighs wide as he found her heat and ran a finger over her softness there.

When his finger dipped inside her quickly, she gasped into the bedspread. Her knees shook as he kneeled between them, then in one quick motion, he embedded himself deep within her.

"Mine," he said against the base of her neck. "Say it," he growled and then ran his tongue up the sweet column of her neck.

"Yes," she moaned and flexed her hips into him.

"Say it, Kristen."

"Yours." She sighed and fisted the bedspread in her hands. "I'm yours." No, that was not what he wanted to hear. He pulled back, and she cried out when he left her.

"Easy." He smiled as she rolled over and tried to tug him back toward her. He nudged her shoulders until she turned and lay in front of him. "I want to hear you say it." He looked down into her sea-green eyes.

"I'm yours," she said, just before nibbling on her bottom lip.

He leaned down and kissed her lips until he felt her relax again. "No." He pulled back and ran a finger over her chin. "I love you."

He watched her eyes clear a little. When she shook her head lightly, he tried not to frown.

"Aiden."

"You know it's there," he said, sliding into her more slowly this time. "You must feel it," he whispered and watched her eyes close and her head fall back. "Feel it here." He pushed deeper inside her and held himself still. "Feel it here." He placed a soft kiss on her lips until she moaned and moved under him.

"Yes," she whispered as she pulled him closer.

"Yes?" He looked back down at her.

She looked up at him and nodded. "Yes, I love you."

He smiled and then started to move with her. Her nails dug into his hips as she held on to him. He said those three words over and over as they spent the entire night pleasing one another. He felt like he could spend a lifetime pleasing her, being with her. He was so thankful that she'd forgiven him, given him a second chance.

♦ ♦ ♦

When the sun came up, the whole house was lit with brightness. They couldn't escape the light if they tried since there were no blinds or curtains on any of the windows.

"I guess there is something to be said for having dark curtains," he said as he threw the blankets over their heads.

"I bet they would spoil the view." She peeked her head out and sighed. "How am I supposed to stay in bed when it's so beautiful out?" She sat up and looked out the windows.

"I know how," he said from under the covers as he ran his hands over her naked body. He heard her moan and then felt her scoot farther down until he had complete access.

An hour later, they were showered and dressed and in the kitchen.

"I'm only here because you promised me waffles." She frowned as she sat on a barstool.

He laughed. "You're so easy."

"Easy? You call making waffles easy?" She motioned toward the kitchen. "Prove it."

Less than fifteen minutes later, he set a plate of huge waffles smothered with strawberries in front of her. "Easy." He poured himself another cup of coffee.

"Who's the easy one? All it took was me challenging you to get you to make me breakfast."

He sat down next to her to eat his own waffles. "How about a hike today?"

"Seriously? With my luck I'd slide down the mountain or something."

"There are no mountains. We're only five minutes into the foothills."

"Where?" she asked.

"Actually, about ten minutes from your folks' place."

"Seriously?" She blinked a few times. "I didn't know anything like this was around."

"The cabin is only four years old."

She shook her head and took another bite of her waffle.

"In that case, I'd be happy to go for a stroll. After all, nothing bad can happen to me if I'm on my home turf."

♦ ♦ ♦

Kristen helped Aiden through the doorway.

"I just didn't see the hole," he said again. She tried not to laugh. She felt bad for him, especially since she'd seen how swollen his ankle was already.

"I'm not carrying you up all those stairs." She nodded to the huge staircase.

"Get me to the sofa. Then I'll need some ice."

"You need a doctor." She frowned at him as she helped him sit down.

"What I need is a couple aspirin and an ice pack." He looked at her until she sighed and walked toward the back to find what he wanted.

When she came back with a frozen blue ice bag and a small bottle of aspirin, he was asleep on the sofa. Setting the ice on his ankle carefully, she covered him with a blanket that had been thrown over the back of a chair, and she lay next to him.

She must have fallen asleep, since the next time she surfaced, it was to Aiden's moans. Her back was covered in sweat and when she reached around, she realized he was burning up.

Pulling the blanket off him, she gasped when she felt his fevered skin.

"Aiden?" She shook his shoulders. He just moaned a little in reply. "Aiden?" She shook him again. When he didn't wake, she rushed over and grabbed her cell phone from her jacket pocket.

She called her father first, but since she didn't know the address of the place, she couldn't tell him where they were.

He tried to talk her down from her hysteria, but it was no use. She was having a full-blown panic attack.

"Look around the place. There's bound to be something with the address on it. A magazine, a newspaper?" her father said.

She'd seen a few magazines in the downstairs bathroom and rushed in there to look.

She read off the address from the back of the woman's magazine. "Dad, he's burning up."

"Get a cold washcloth on him. I'll be there in a shake." Her father hung up as she rushed back out to sit by Aiden.

When she placed the cold washcloth on his head, he started shaking and tried to push her hand away from him.

"No, Aiden. I've got to cool you off." She felt tears sliding down her face.

"Krissy." His eyes opened a little. "I'm sorry, babe." He reached for her. "I should have told you everything."

She sighed and held him close. "Hush now, it's all over." She felt him shivering in her arms.

"No, I almost lost you. I don't want to ever lose you," he mumbled next to her skin. "I was going to give it to you tonight." His body jerked.

"What?" she said, placing a kiss on his heated forehead.

"The ring." He moaned. "We were going to have dinner under the stars on the patio. I was going to ask you then." When she looked down at him, his eyes were still closed and his face had turned bright red.

"Aiden?" She shook him, trying to rouse him.

"I'm sorry," he kept saying over and over again.

There was a quick knock on the door, then her father and mother rushed in. Her father had a small first-aid bag under his arm that he always kept in the trunk of his car.

"What happened?" he asked as he sat next to Aiden's warm body. Her mother wrapped her arms around Kristen. She felt herself start to shake.

She told them about their walk and how he'd stepped in a hole and twisted his ankle.

When her father pulled up his jeans and exposed his ankle, she almost passed out. Instead of a small bruise, his leg was dark purplish-black. There were long red streaks that ran down his foot.

"Kate, call 911." Her father looked over to her mother.

"Dad?" She dropped her arms and rushed to Aiden's side.

"It looks like a small snakebite. It must have been a snake hole he stepped in. It could be a rattlesnake bite. We won't know until we get him to the hospital."

She felt her heart stop and everything started to go white before her father pushed her down to the chair and shoved her head between her legs.

"Damn it, Kristen, I don't need you passing out just now."

She took a few deep breaths and then glanced up at Aiden.

"How long ago did he get bit?" he asked.

She glanced at the clock on the wall. "An hour."

"It's not acting like a rattlesnake bite, then. We might be out of the woods." He propped Aiden's chest up by piling the throw pillows behind him. "Has he been sick?" he asked as he leaned down to listen to him breath.

"N-n-no. Just feverish. His ankle hurt at first. But he came in and fell asleep." She closed her eyes and wished she'd looked at his leg more closely. "I put some ice on it." She nodded to the melted pack.

It seemed to take forever for the ambulance to get there. In that time, she'd called his parents and told them what was going on. They told her they would meet her at the hospital in Golden.

Finally, the ambulance arrived. She watched as they loaded Aiden into the back. He had yet to wake up, which only worried her more.

Her mother had rushed upstairs and grabbed their bags and thrown them in the back of their car. Kristen rode in the backseat as her parents followed the ambulance down the hills into Golden.

She'd been to the hospital several times growing up but had never expected to be there with him. Not like this.

When they walked into the ER, Aiden's family was already there waiting.

"Kristen." Amber rushed over to her and hugged her. "We saw them cart him in." She nodded to the large glass window. "Mom and Dad were going to see if they could find out anything more, but they told us we had to wait."

She let Amber lead her over to a row of chairs.

"Hi, I'm Amber." She waved at Kristen's parents. "Aiden's sister. This is Ashley and my parents, Ann and Eric."

Her parents introduced themselves and everyone shook hands.

"Dad's an MD. Family medicine," Kristen said in between taking big gulps of air.

"I've got some pull around here. I'll see if I can find anything out." Her father walked toward the nurses' station.

"I should have called sooner," she said to herself.

"Honey, it's okay. You didn't know." Ann sat next to her and wrapped an arm around her. Kristen could see the tears falling down her face through her own watery eyes.

"Good news and bad news." Her father walked over a few minutes later. "It's not a snakebite."

"What's the bad news?" She stood up.

"Looks like a black widow bite. They're treating him now with anti-venin. They say he's lucky it wasn't a brown recluse bite."

She shivered. "How can they tell?"

"They have their ways." Her father shook his head. "Hate those damn things. Pardon." He nodded his head to Aiden's mother. "We should know something soon. They say two people can go back to his room now."

"Kristen, why don't you and I head back first," Ann said, taking her arm.

She followed Aiden's mother through several doors. When they walked into the small glass room where Aiden was, she was surprised to see him sitting up, eyes wide, looking worried.

"Hey." He reached for her, and when she rushed into his arms, he held her while she cried. "It's okay. I'm okay," he kept saying over and over again into her hair.

"I was just so scared of losing you," she said against his skin. Just feeling his strong arms around her helped the fear subside. She never wanted to feel that scared about losing him again. For a moment, she thought about blaming her bad luck once again, then squared her shoulders and remembered that she was making her own luck now.

CHAPTER TWENTY-TWO

Aiden was trying to keep it together for Kristen's sake. His foot and ankle stung like they were on fire, but when he was holding Kristen, he could only think about her.

He wanted to tell Kristen how he felt, what his plans were, but since his mother was there alongside her, he settled for letting Kristen sit beside him on the bed.

"They gave me a shot of something that broke the fever"—he snapped his fingers—"like that." He smiled. "Now they're shoving some antivenin in me. I guess I should have let you call the doctor." He chuckled and then frowned when he noticed the joke hadn't cheered Kristen up. "Mom, can you give us a minute?"

"Sure, honey." She leaned down and placed a kiss on his forehead. "We're all just outside if you need us."

"Thanks." His eyes didn't leave Kristen's.

When Ann left, Kristen burst into tears and leaned her head against his chest. He held on to her as she cried it out.

"Hey, it's okay." He brushed her hair with his hand. When a nurse popped her head in the doorway, he waved her in.

Kristen heard her and tried to sit up, but he held her still.

"This is Nurse . . ." he started.

"Kelly," she supplied. "I'm just checking Mr. Scott's vitals and drawing some blood really quick." He looked down at Kristen, who used the tissue Kelly handed her.

They sat in silence as the nurse got everything done. When the woman finally walked out, Kristen's eyes had dried up and she was no longer pale and pasty looking.

"I was so scared," she whispered once they were alone again.

"So was I there for a while. I couldn't make sense of anything. I couldn't surface from the heat. I heard you . . ." He pulled her closer. "And knew I had to fight the darkness for you."

Tears fell down her cheeks again.

"Don't cry." He wiped them with his fingers. "Look." He pointed to his ankle. "The swelling is already going down and I can feel my toes again."

"Next time you ask me to go walking, you'd better mean to the coffee shop and back," she teased.

"That's a deal."

Just then there was a knock on the door.

"Hello?" A short Asian man walked in. "I'm Dr. Yee." The man glanced down at a chart. "I hear we had a fight with a spider."

"Looks that way." He nodded to his foot.

"Oh yeah. You're lucky." The older man smiled at them. "Some people can't take the venom. For others"—he shrugged—"it's no big deal." He held up his finger. "I've been bitten three times. On the same finger." He held up his hand. "Only gave me a headache." He chuckled. "We'll want to keep an eye on you for a little while, make sure the antivenin is working. Most likely you can leave within the hour." He tapped Aiden on his other leg. "Any questions?" He looked between the two of them.

"Um." Kristen sniffled a little. "If this happens again, what should I do next time?"

"Well, since he's proven that he doesn't like black widow venom, I'd say get him to a doctor or hospital as soon as you can. Most cases, you'll see fever, nausea, pain, headaches. In worse cases, you can have shock, high blood pressure. It's a good thing you brought him in when you did."

He walked over and took a closer look at the bite, making sure not to touch the swollen area. "You'll want to keep this area clean. If the swelling doesn't go away completely in a few days, come back in and we will lance the rest of the poison out of it."

Aiden felt Kristen shiver.

"Thanks," he said and shook the man's hand. "I'll be sure to keep an eye on it."

"You do that. You two have a nice day, and don't let this spoil your weekend." He waved. "Gorgeous day out there."

"Yes, yes, it is," Aiden said as the man left.

Just then his mother walked back in. "Was that the doctor?" She walked over and stood next to his bed.

"I'll go fill everyone in outside." Kristen stood up quickly, but he tugged on her hand and pulled her back down for a quick kiss.

"Don't go anywhere. Okay?" he said.

"Just try and get rid of me."

He smiled as she walked out.

"I like her," his mother said as she sat next to him. "Did you get a chance to pop the question?"

He frowned and shook his head. "No, I was going to do it tonight." He leaned back and sighed. His energy was quickly fading. "I guess this ruined everything."

"It doesn't have to." She patted his hand. "Eric proposed to me on our flight back from Phoenix."

He smiled, remembering it. "That's different."

"Oh?" Her blonde eyebrows shot up. "I suppose you're more in love with her than Eric is with me?" She put her hands on her hips.

He laughed. "No, I just have more couth than Eric."

She slapped his arm and giggled. He knew he'd blown his first chance at making the most romantic move ever, but at least he still had time to fix it.

♦ ♦ ♦

Kristen sat in the back of her parents' car next to Aiden as they drove them toward his place.

"I'm sorry our time in the cabin was ruined." He played with her hand, rubbing his fingers next to hers. The friction was driving her nuts, and she wanted nothing more than to be alone with him.

"It's okay." She shrugged. "At least for once it wasn't me in distress."

"I told you, we make our own luck," he replied.

She nodded. "I'm beginning to believe that."

They sat in silence as they hit afternoon traffic.

"Your family seems very nice," her father said, glancing back at them.

"Thanks. It's not the first meeting I'd hoped for, but I guess it worked." He smiled.

"Your sisters are beautiful. Is it true that Amber is going to play Glinda in *Wicked* next month?"

"Yes. I can get you a deal on tickets, if you want. Kristen and I have front-row seats, opening night."

"We do?" She glanced at him and saw him wince.

"It was going to be a surprise." He shrugged. "Surprise."

"It's a wonderful surprise." She leaned over and kissed him. When she noticed him flinch a little, she leaned back and looked down at his foot, which was propped across her lap with an ice pack over the wrappings.

"We'd love to go, wouldn't we, Hank?" Her mother slapped at her father's arm and smiled at him.

"Love to." He looked over at his wife. "I'll see about getting us tickets for our anniversary."

Her mother blushed and smiled at him. It was funny—a month ago, she would have been embarrassed by how her parents acted like love-struck teenagers, but now, it just seemed right.

Her parents helped them up to his condo. Her mother carried their bags as Kristen and her father helped Aiden walk the short distance to the elevator.

When the doors shut, no sense of panic came over her. Instead, she stayed focused on Aiden and got through the long ride up to his floor without so much as a hitch.

Once Aiden was settled on his sofa with a fresh ice pack on his foot, her parents left them alone.

"Could you hand me my bag?" he asked after he'd swallowed his pills.

She nodded and then stopped and sat next to him. "I have something I want to say first." She took his hands in hers. "You scared me today," she said against his skin, holding him tight. "I know I said the words to you, but something kept fighting inside of me, causing me not to believe in myself. In my feelings. Not until I saw you . . ." She closed her eyes. "I hadn't realized how much I loved you. Not until then. Aiden Scott, I love you with every ounce of my being."

"I love you too," he said.

"You may not remember, but while you were feverish, you said some things." She smiled when she saw the frown form on his lips. She knew exactly why he wanted his bag and what was hiding in the side pocket. "And I've had some time to think about my answer." She could see him holding his breath. "And it's yes."

He blinked a few times and then pulled her closer. "This isn't how I wanted to do this."

"I know, you told me." She reached down and moved his bag closer, then pulled out the silver box from the side pocket that he'd talked about during his fever. "Here." She handed it to him. "Ask me."

He looked down at his leg, which was propped up with three pillows. "Well, so much for getting down on one knee." He took her hand in his.

She felt her knees go weak. If she hadn't been sitting beside him, she would have fallen to the floor.

"Kristen, I've never met a woman like you before. You have the legs of a goddess, the brain of a surgeon, the humor of a world-class comedian." He smiled. "The lips of . . ."

She chuckled. "I get the point."

His eyes went soft. "You're the love of my life. My best friend. I can't imagine spending a day or night without you. Will you marry me?" She knew he was waiting for her answer.

Deciding that it was time, she forced her life to take a turn toward good luck and answered.

"I thought you'd never ask. Yes, of course I'll marry you."

EPILOGUE

A few months later, Kristen stood at the large windows and watched the first snow slowly fall over the city. She wrapped her arms tighter around herself, happy to be warm in her yoga pants and a thick sweater.

When Aiden's arms came around her, she sighed and rested her head back against his chest.

"Happy?" His rich voice sounded next to her ear.

She nodded lightly. "More than I ever dreamed I'd be."

He pulled her closer. "Tomorrow's the first day in the new building."

She turned toward him, wrapping her arms around his shoulders. "Nervous?" she asked. He looked comfortable in an old pair of jeans and a worn sweatshirt.

He shook his head slightly. "Excited is more like it."

She took his face into her hands. "That makes two of us."

He smiled and brushed a finger down her cheek. "You aren't nervous about impressing your new boss?"

She laughed. "Not in the least." Reaching up, she placed her lips on his and felt her entire body relax.

"I know he's going to love me, more than I'd ever dreamed possible."

SNEAK PEEK AT *Sweet Resolve*, THE

NEXT BOOK IN THE LUCKY SERIES

Coming Summer 2016

Amelia rushed through her front door, almost knocking over her little brother, Joel. Instead, she ended up falling backward and landing on her butt, hard. The pain shot up her back, causing the tears that had been in her eyes to flood down her cheeks. After quickly yelling at him to get out of her way, she bolted up the stairs and slammed her bedroom door shut behind her.

She threw her bag across the room and leaned against her door, wincing when she bumped her bruised backside on the door handle. She knew it wasn't her little brother's fault that she'd fallen down. She hadn't seen him because her eyes had been too full of unshed tears. Just the thought of the boy who had caused her the ultimate embarrassment had her vibrating with anger.

Closing her eyes, she flipped around and rested her forehead against her bedroom door as more tears washed down her cheeks. She'd never been so humiliated before. It had been his mission to embarrass her ever since he'd moved in down the street during her kindergarten year.

It wasn't as if her life would have been all peaches and cream even if she weren't being bullied by a boy half her size. She sighed and opened her eyes to look around her room. There were still boxes shoved in the corner and piled high in her closet.

She had been awakened in the middle of the night a few days ago by the sounds of her mother packing up all her things. "Mom, what are you doing?" Amelia had asked groggily.

"Oh, Amy," her mother croaked out her nickname. Her mom had rushed over to her, crying as she tried to explain. But she hadn't made any sense sitting next to Amy babbling as tears rolled down her face. But then Amy had heard one word she did understand. *Divorce.* Even though she was only eleven, she'd felt much older after her mother told her that she and her father were getting a divorce.

When what was happening finally registered in her sleepy mind, she'd instantly thought of Kristen, her best friend in the whole world. They'd known each other since kindergarten. She couldn't possibly move away from Kristen. Amy had begged and pleaded with her mother that night while the distraught woman had rushed around tossing clothes and items into boxes.

Finally, her father had walked in and taken her mother's arm, and together they had left the room. Her father had glanced back at Amy as she cried on the edge of her bed.

"It's okay, sweetie. Go back to sleep. We'll talk about all this in the morning." Her father's voice had soothed her then.

Less than a month later, her father had moved into a small apartment in downtown Golden, Colorado. Even though her parents still weren't officially divorced, she found it difficult to get over the fear that, at some point, her mother would sweep in and finish packing up her things and they would move far away. Because of this, she'd kept everything in boxes, unsure of what would happen next.

Amy walked over and flung herself on her bed. But, as bad as her family life was, it still didn't scratch the surface of what had been done to her on the bus ride home. Her back teeth clenched at the mere thought of him.

He teased her about everything. For the past couple of years it had been her height. Amy was tall for her age—she was taller than most of her girlfriends, which meant that she towered a foot above all the boys in her class also.

She rolled over and hugged her pillow to her belly. Her silent tears slid across the bridge of her nose and fell to her pillowcase.

Kristen would have normally been there to defend her against the bully, but her friend's parents had picked her up early that day for a dentist appointment. Amy wished she'd been the one to go to the dentist instead. She hated this boy more than going to Dr. Stein's office.

By tomorrow morning, everyone in her entire school would know what he'd done to her. Then there would be no stopping the flood of humiliation that was sure to follow her all week long. All of a sudden, moving away didn't seem so bad.

She glanced down at the boxes, then over at the picture of her and Kristen on her nightstand. Shaking her head, she decided that nothing could ever be bad enough for her to move away and give up her best friend. Especially anything Logan Miller could ever do to her.

ABOUT THE AUTHOR

Photo © 2015 Daryl Sanders

Jill Sanders is *The New York Times* and *USA Today* bestselling author of the Pride, Secret, West, and Grayton Series romance novels. She continues to lure new readers with her sweet and sexy stories. Her books are available in every English-speaking country as audiobooks and are now being translated into six different languages.

Born as an identical twin to a large family, she was raised in the Pacific Northwest and later relocated to Colorado for college and a successful IT career before discovering her talent as a writer. She now makes her home along the Emerald Coast in Florida where she enjoys the beach, hiking, swimming, wine-tasting, and of course writing.

Connect with Jill on Facebook: www.fb.com/JillSandersBooks
Twitter: @JillMSanders or visit her Web site at www.JillSanders.com